Mistletoe!

For her entire stay she'd managed to steer clear of Richard. Till now. Molly's eyes followed his glance up to the mistletoe in the doorway and she knew she'd been caught.

Before she could move away, Richard kissed her. It wasn't a friendly peck. No, his kiss was skillful and deep, unlike any she'd experienced. His arms were like iron around her, his aftershave like a love potion drawing her in....

Dangerous, screamed an inner voice, breaking the trance.

Molly pulled back, stuttered out a breathy "G-Good night" and bolted up the stairs as if a bogeyman was after her.

But no bogeyman kissed like Richard Anderson....

JUDY CHRISTENBERRY

This is Judy's 75th book!

Step into a world where family counts,
men are strong and true to their word—
and where romance always wins the day!

Judy's stories are guaranteed to
make you feel good!

Judy Christenberry delivers:

"A hero every woman will want, blended with...
remarkable storytelling."
—*Romantic Times BOOKclub*

JUDY CHRISTENBERRY
Her Christmas Wedding Wish

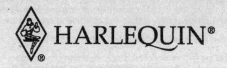

HARLEQUIN®

TORONTO • NEW YORK • LONDON
AMSTERDAM • PARIS • SYDNEY • HAMBURG
STOCKHOLM • ATHENS • TOKYO • MILAN • MADRID
PRAGUE • WARSAW • BUDAPEST • AUCKLAND

ISBN-13: 978-0-373-03919-7
ISBN-10:   0-373-03919-0

HER CHRISTMAS WEDDING WISH

First North American Publication 2006.

Copyright © 2006 by Judy Russell Christenberry.

This edition published by arrangement with Harlequin Books S.A.

www.eHarlequin.com

Printed in U.S.A.

Judy Christenberry has been writing romances for fifteen years because she loves happy endings as much as her readers do. A former French teacher, Judy now devotes herself to writing full-time. She hopes readers have as much fun reading her stories as she does writing them. She spends her spare time reading, watching her favorite sports teams and keeping track of her two daughters. Judy's a native Texan, but now lives in Arizona.

In February look out for Judy's next heartwarming romance in our brand-new WESTERN WEDDINGS series,

Rancher and Protector

Only from Harlequin Romance®

CHAPTER ONE

MOLLY SODERLING hurried back down the hall to the one patient who had been on her mind all through her break. Toby Astin. The eight-year-old had also found his way into her heart, ever since he'd come into the hospital three days ago, the victim of a car crash. The same crash that had killed his parents and two other adults, and had left the boy an orphan. Less than a month before Christmas.

Molly's heart ached for him. She knew exactly what he was feeling, as she, too, had lost her parents when she was a young child. She remembered how lonely she was the first Christmas without them, and every one since then.

In Toby's eyes she saw the loss he suffered; in his clinging arms she felt his pain. In the three days he'd been here, no one had come for him. Perhaps after the funerals someone would claim him. She didn't want Toby to be put into the foster care system as she had been.

As she turned down the pediatric wing, she saw two people clad in black enter his room. Perhaps they were mourners who'd attended the funeral for his parents today. According to his doctor, Toby's uncle and grandmother had phoned to ask for Toby to attend, but Dr. Bradford had refused.

He was concerned the boy might suffer depression.

Molly had disagreed with the doctor, but he wasn't going to listen to her. Having had to attend her parents' funeral when she was seven, she knew how comforting it had been to see others mourning their deaths also.

Molly sighed. Then, forcing a smile on her face, she turned into Toby's room.

"Molly!" he cried as if she were a lifesaver.

"Hi, Toby. Did you eat your dinner?"

"Yes, but—"

"Are you his nurse?" the man in the black suit asked abruptly, stepping toward her. He looked about thirty, with dark hair and striking blue eyes.

"I'm one of Toby's nurses."

"He seems extraordinarily attached to you."

Was it condemnation she heard in his voice? Her shoulders stiffened. "We've become friends," she said tersely.

Then she turned her attention to Toby. "Can I get you anything, honey?"

"I'd like some ice cream," he said hesitantly, shooting a look at the man as if he would object.

"Sure. I'll be right back with it."

She passed the older woman dressed in a black designer suit, leaning against the wall. She wasn't sure who the elegant-looking woman was. Maybe a family friend or maybe even the grandmother she'd heard mentioned. But no, she wasn't acting like a grandmother, at least none Molly had ever imagined.

"Excuse me, Ms. Soderling," the man called.

How did he know her name? Molly turned around. "Yes, sir?"

"We're taking Toby with us in the morning."

Before he could go on, Molly said, "I'm sorry to see him go. I'll miss him. Are you his guardian?"

"Yes, by default."

She stared at him, her eyebrows raised. Who would say such a thing, as if the boy was nothing more than a burden to be endured?

"The other couple, who also died in the car with Toby's parents, were named in their will as guardians. However, my mother and I are his only relatives. I'm an attorney and I filed the papers this morning to be named guardian. They've assured me it would be approved. I want to get Toby home so he can begin to heal."

"Good. He's been feeling lost since no one had come to claim him."

"The doctor in charge of Toby says he's very fond of you."

Molly frowned. "Yes, I told you we've become friends."

"He's eight years old. How could you be friends?"

Molly said nothing, turning to continue on her way.

"Wait!"

She didn't like the order, but she obeyed. No need to irritate the man if he was going away in the morning. "Yes?"

"Dr. Bradford said you didn't have any family here."

"Why would Dr. Bradford tell you that?" she asked carefully.

"Because I need someone to come with us to Dallas to take care of Toby and help him settle in."

"Sir, I'm a pediatric nurse, not a baby-sitter."

"I know. And I'm willing to pay your going rate, twenty-four hours a day, if you'll come with us in the morning."

"For how long?" she asked, startled at his offering.

"For a month. You'll make more than three times your salary, Ms. Soderling."

"I don't know if the hospital—"

"Dr. Bradford assured me he could spare you."

Molly didn't know what to think. "I'll have to talk to Dr. Bradford."

"He left a note for you at the nurses' station," the man said, as if that alone should persuade her.

He expected her to drop everything and go to Dallas for a month, as if it were nothing but a shift reassignment. Not that she had anything holding her here in Florida, especially at holiday time. Still, the man hadn't even introduced himself! "Excuse me, sir, but who are you exactly?"

"I'm Richard Anderson, Toby's uncle." As he spoke, he stood straighter, his shoulders back in a proud gesture. But he made no move to shake her hand.

Neither did Molly. "I'll go read the note," she said. And she walked away.

At the nurses' station, she got the Dixie cup of ice cream for Toby and asked the nurse on duty if Dr. Bradford had left a note for her.

"Oh, yeah. Sorry, Molly. I forgot to give it to you."

"Thanks, Ellen," Molly said, taking the note with her as she found a quiet corner of the floor to read it.

Indeed, Dr. Bradford had asked her to go with the Andersons to Dallas. Because of her rapport with little Toby, he thought her best for the job. He'd approved a month's leave for her if she decided to go. And, she guessed, to make her refusal harder, he added that Mr. Anderson had offered two hundred thousand dollars to the pediatric wing if the hospital could supply a nurse for the boy.

That much money could help the children, Molly knew. And she knew Dr. Bradford was counting on her love of the kids…

But a month in Dallas with the seemingly pompous Richard Anderson? Could she handle it? The assignment would span the holidays, and aside from some volunteer work, she had no Christmas plans. At the very least she wouldn't have to spend another Christmas alone. She could stand the thought of that. And she'd be with Toby.

Still unsure, she pocketed the note and brought the boy his ice cream. "Your wish is my command," she joked to Toby as she pulled the lid off the Dixie cup and held it out to him.

Though his arm and collarbone were in casts, he could hold the Dixie cup in his injured hand and eat with his right.

"Thank you, Molly. You're not going to leave, are you?"

The boy's sad blue eyes reached right down into her heart. "No, sweetie, I'll stay for a little while." She smiled as she pulled up a chair next to the bed. His frown transformed into a broad grin and he dug into his ice cream. How could she leave him? Not just now, but when he went with his uncle and grandmother?

"What's wrong, Molly?" Toby asked anxiously.

Molly knew her concerns were nothing compared to the tragedy Toby had experienced. She pasted a bright smile on her lips. "Nothing, sweetheart. Hey, would you like me to go with you to Dallas, where your uncle lives?"

"You could do that? And stay forever?" Toby asked, hope in his voice.

"No, but I could go and stay for a few weeks, during Christmas. Wouldn't that be fun?"

"Oh, yeah," Toby said, reaching up to hug her neck.

With his face buried in her hair, he whispered, "I don't want to go with them."

"I know, sweetie, but we'll be together and I'll help you."

"Okay," Toby agreed as he pulled back to look at her. "You'll really come with me?"

"Yes, your uncle has asked me to come." She settled the little boy back in his bed. "Now, eat your ice cream before it melts while I talk to your uncle."

And just like that, her mind was made up.

She stood and walked over to the man watching them with no sign of emotion. "I'll take the job, Mr. Anderson. When were you planning on leaving?"

"We have seats on an eleven o'clock flight tomorrow morning. We'll need to leave for the airport by nine, which means you should be here by eight to get Toby ready."

"Does Toby have clothes?" The shirt and pants the boy had been wearing had been bloodied and torn.

The man stared at her, as if he hadn't comprehended her question.

"Toby hasn't had any clothes since he arrived and we cut off his bloody ones. He'll need clothes for the trip."

With a weary sigh, the man said, "Of course. It'll take a little while because I've got to get my mother back to the hotel. But then I'll go to his house and pack his clothes."

Molly knew she was a sucker for the weary and down-trodden, but she couldn't help herself. "If you want, I could meet you there and help you pack up his things. It would save you a trip back to the hospital."

After a moment's hesitation, Richard Anderson nodded. "I'll take that offer. Thank you." He looked at his watch. "Can you meet me there at eight o'clock?"

"Yes, but I don't know the address."

He pulled a card and a pen out of his pocket and wrote an address on the back of the card. "Do you know where this is?"

Molly nodded. The address was actually close to her apartment. How strange. She'd lived just a few blocks from Toby. "Yes, I do."

"Then I'll see you there at eight o'clock."

Molly heard a warning in his voice not to be late. But she was always on time. With a nod, the man took his mother's arm and left Toby's room.

That was when Molly realized the older woman had remained in the back of the room the entire time. She hadn't taken a seat nor uttered a word to her grandson. Instantly Molly felt good about her decision. How could she have let this sweet boy go with these cold-hearted people?

Molly came back to Toby's side. "Was the ice cream good?"

"Yes. Are you really going to go with me tomorrow?" the little boy asked anxiously.

"Yes, I told you I would. And I'll be there all through Christmas. I've never been to Dallas. Have you?"

"No. I never met my uncle and my grandmother before."

How could that be? Molly wondered. They were family. But for Toby's sake, she tried to put a positive spin on it. "Well, you'll get a chance to know them now." She grinned. "I have to go if I'm going to be ready to leave in the morning. Ellen will come in and see you before you go to sleep. Okay?"

"Okay. You really are going with me?"

"Yes, Toby. I'll be here in the morning, I promise."

* * *

Richard Anderson pulled up to his sister's home in a nice neighborhood in Jacksonville, Florida. He dreaded going in the house. He'd missed Susan after her move to Florida. He'd talked to her on the phone some, but it hadn't been the same.

Nine years ago his father had been furious with his daughter. He'd blown up at her and had refused any consideration of reconciliation. Now it was too late for both of them. James Anderson had been a brilliant man, but when it came to his daughter he had been foolish. He'd lost her because of his anger, long before either of them had died.

When another car pulled up behind him, Richard automatically checked his watch. Good. The nurse was on time. It would be easier to enter the house with a stranger.

He got out of his car and waited until the nurse joined him. "I appreciate you coming, Ms. Soderling."

"Please call me Molly, and I'm glad I can be of assistance."

"My mother would've come, but the past few days have been hard on her."

"Of course. Shall we go in?"

Richard pulled the keys from his pocket. They had been handed to him by the funeral director, along with other items found in the clothing. He selected one that he hoped would open the door.

He'd guessed right. The door swung open and he followed the nurse into the house. He was hit almost at once with a wave of grief. The house showed so much of Susan. It was warm and cozy, a home where a family shared and loved.

He turned to the nurse, hoping to control his grief, and he saw the same reaction on her face. She hadn't even known Susan.

"Poor Toby," she muttered.

"Why would you say that?"

"Because I can see what he's lost," she said quietly, and he saw the sheen of moisture in her eyes.

Before he could think of anything to say, she said, "We'd better get started. Do you know where Toby's bedroom is?"

He shook his head. "I've never been here."

"Oh. Then I'll go look for it."

Richard decided he should remove any valuables his sister and her husband had before he hired someone to come pack up the house. What would he do with everything? What would Toby want to keep? Hard decisions to make on the spur of the moment.

He entered the master bedroom, neat and tidy, like Susan. And hard for him to enter. He looked in the closet and found his sister's jewelry box. Then he found a folder of their financial papers on her husband's side of the closet, and some cuff links and things in a small leather box. He assumed Toby would one day want them.

"Mr. Anderson?"

Molly appeared in the doorway of the bedroom. "Yes? And please, call me Richard."

"Am I packing everything Toby has or just enough for the trip?"

"Have you found any luggage?"

"Yes, it's stored in the third bedroom closet."

"Then please take everything you can, packing the immediate needs in the smallest bag. I'll be there to help you in a moment."

After she left the room, Richard realized how extraordinarily kind she had been to come with him and do the grisly task. It was like sorting through the bones. A very personal experience.

As soon as he'd gathered anything valuable, he carried it all to Toby's room. It was a perfect bedroom for a little boy.

Susan had loved her child. It showed in so many ways.

He stood there, not wanting to enter. Molly was folding clothes and putting them in the bags. He had to force himself to join her. "I need to put these things in one of the larger bags," he said, nodding down to the articles he held.

"Of course. If it's anything valuable, you should put them in a carry-on bag so you can keep them safe."

He frowned. "I guess you're right."

She pointed out a small bag he could use. When he got to the hotel, he could transfer it to his own carry-on bag or his mother's.

By the time he had those things stowed away, Molly had finished packing Toby's clothes. Then she packed some books from a nearby shelf.

"The packers will get those things," Richard said.

"I know, but I thought it would help Toby if he had some things of his own with him."

Richard agreed. Molly was very thoughtful.

"I can't thank you enough for coming with me to the house, Molly. It was difficult to—to come here."

"Yes, I know."

Molly reached for one more thing. A small framed picture of Toby with his parents. It sat on his bedside table.

He watched her but said nothing.

She was an attractive woman, he suddenly realized. Her

reddish-brown hair was shoulder length and simply styled. Her green eyes held so much sympathy, he didn't like to meet her glance. When she smiled, as she had at Toby, her face lit up a room. No wonder the boy was attached to her. She was like a warm fire on a cold night.

He backed away, recognizing a danger there. And he'd invited her to his home for a month. Was he crazy? No, just desperate. He had to protect his mother. Since his father's death eighteen months ago the not-yet-sixty-year-old had aged. She leaned on him, so needy in many ways. Now she had to deal with her daughter's death and the regrets she had.

How could she deal with an eight-year-old boy? And the child was frightened, since he didn't know them. Molly was the answer to both those problems. He'd made the right move hiring her.

"Uh, I really appreciate your help, Molly," he said again, preparing to set the tone for her visit.

"It's all right, Richard. I'm glad I could help."

"Yes. What I wanted to say is my mother is weak. She won't be able to deal with Toby. I'll need you to shield her from the boy's energy, as well as care for Toby. Will that be a problem?"

She seemed taken aback. But she raised her chin and said coolly, "No, that won't be a problem."

He'd upset her. Too bad. He had to protect his own. "Good. I work long hours, so I won't be there to make sure she's not disturbed, so I will appreciate your help. If there are problems, bring them to me, not my mother."

"Certainly," she said, her voice crisp.

"Are we finished?"

"Yes, of course."

He picked up the two big bags and she grabbed the overnight bag where she packed Toby's things for tomorrow. She also picked up the bag that held the valuables.

"I can get that," he hurriedly said.

The sympathy that had prompted her to come with Richard tonight was drying up. Molly glared at him and set the bag on the floor. Did he think she was going to steal something? "Fine."

She walked back into the living area of the house. The Christmas tree looked forlorn in the darkened room. Suddenly Molly stopped. "The presents. Should we—"

"We don't have room," was his clipped response.

Molly forced herself to keep moving to the front door. Every step she took was a betrayal to Toby. She could feel him protesting. The presents under the tree would be something he needed, not for what was in them, but for the memories associated with them.

"When will their belongings arrive in Dallas?" she asked.

"I don't know. I'll have to make arrangements tonight."

He sounded irritated.

Molly mentally shrugged. She'd done her best for Toby. She couldn't do any more because the man behind her didn't want her to.

She'd thought perhaps he was sad and exhausted at the hospital. Now he seemed surly and difficult. And she was going to live with him for a month? She must be crazy. At least he would be at work most of the time.

Poor Toby, in a house with a grandmother who needed to be protected from him, and an uncle who was never there. He'd gone from a loving home to what? A museum?

She would only be there a month, but she'd do everything she could to make a warm home for Toby.

She squared her shoulders as she marched out to her car. She wasn't going to worry about the man behind her, carrying most of the luggage. That was his choice.

After putting the small case in her car, she turned to look at Richard Anderson, who was loading the rest of the luggage in the trunk of his car.

"I'll see you at the hospital in the morning," she called.

"At nine o'clock. Please be on time. We don't want to run late getting to the airport."

With disdain, she replied, "I'm always on time, Richard."

Then she went back to her car, got in and drove away, leaving him standing there. So what if he didn't like her abrupt withdrawal. He shouldn't have been so snippy.

Immediately she felt remorse for her attitude. The evening had to have been difficult for him, even if he hadn't seen his sister in a while. And it must've been a long day, as she'd guessed at the hospital. She chastised herself for not showing more patience.

But Toby was a little boy. The man and his mother hadn't shown much compassion to him. Richard's concern had been for his mother.

The next few days would be difficult for Toby. But at least he would have her so he wouldn't feel alone. Richard might regret his invitation, but he wasn't going to get rid of her now, even if he wanted to.

She was going to be there for Toby.

For just a little while, and regardless of the heartache when she had to leave, she and Toby would be a family.

* * *

Molly was used to getting up early, but apparently her patient was not. She had to practically dress Toby without any assistance from him. "Toby, you're not helping me, you know."

"But I don't want to go," he said in a low voice. "Mommy and Daddy are—" He cut off on a sob.

Molly put her arms around him. "Sweetie, your mommy and daddy's bodies are buried here, but *they* will always be with you, in your heart. You just have to think about them and they'll come to you in your heart and in your memory."

"Really?"

"Yes, and one day, when you're older, you can come back to visit their graves. But they won't be there, because they'll be with you, in your heart."

Toby patted his heart. "Do you think they're here now?"

"Yes, I do. And they want the best for you."

"So you think they want me to go with my uncle?"

"Yes, because he'll take care of you. That's important."

"Okay," Toby agreed with a sigh.

"Good. Let's get your shirt on. I like it. It matches your eyes."

"That's what Mommy said, but I like it because it's easy to wear."

Molly smiled. "I see."

Once she got his shoes on him, she helped Toby get down from his bed. He had a cast on his left collarbone that ended on the upper part of his arm and the cast on his lower arm started just below his elbow. At least he was mobile.

She managed to get him discharged from the hospital and down at the front door five minutes early. She already knew Richard would be irritated if they were late.

Her bags were down by the door. She'd left them with

one of the greeters so she wouldn't have to drag them upstairs and down. She sat Toby down in one of the chairs for visitors and hurried over to get her bags.

"Molly!" Toby cried urgently.

Molly whirled around.

Toby was pointing to his uncle coming through the door.

"I'm coming, Toby," she called. Gathering her two bags, she rushed across the lobby to meet Richard at Toby's side. "We're ready," she announced.

"Good. Toby, can you walk?"

"Yes," the little boy said, his eyes big.

"Okay. I'll get your bag. May I take one of yours, Molly?"

"No, thank you. I can manage." She followed the two males out the door, keeping an eye on Toby. The boy kept looking over his shoulder at Molly, to be sure she was following.

Toby's grandmother was sitting in the front seat. Elizabeth Anderson smoothed back her graying hair and turned her blue eyes to Molly. The woman looked rested, Molly thought. She was glad someone was. She had just come off the night shift for the last six months and was still adjusting to working in the daylight.

She got in the back seat with Toby, wondering if his uncle was still irritated with her. Judging by his silence as he loaded the trunk, he probably was. Richard Anderson didn't appear to be the forgiving kind.

Toby sat very still as Molly put his seat belt on him. "Can she speak?" he whispered, nodding toward his grandmother.

"I don't know," Molly returned. After all, she hadn't heard the woman utter a sound, either.

"Is everything all right?" Richard asked, looking at them in the rearview mirror.

"Yes, Richard."

Before Molly could stop him, Toby leaned forward and said, "Are you my grandma?"

The woman seemed to freeze.

Richard answered for her. "Yes," he said in clipped tones.

Molly put a hand on Toby's good arm, warning him not to speak again. She didn't believe the woman was as frail as Richard believed, but she was certainly suffering grief at her daughter's death. That was enough for Molly to cut her some slack. For a while.

There was no conversation in the car. All the way to the airport, Molly held Toby's hand and squeezed it when he sent her a panicky look.

When they got out at the airport, Richard got a skycap to take care of their luggage. Then he turned to Molly. "Here are the tickets for the three of you. Please take care of my mother and Toby while I return the rental car. I'll meet you at the gate."

"All right." She nodded to the skycap who led them to the check-in line. She discovered they were flying first class, which made it possible to bypass the long line. In no time, she had checked them in.

"My son—" Mrs. Anderson said, looking as panicky as Toby.

"He'll be joining us at the gate, ma'am. He has to present his own ID, you know. Airport security."

"Oh, yes. Do you—do you know where our gate is?"

"Yes, ma'am. If you'll come with Toby and me, I have our tickets and I can find the gate. It's right over here."

Molly led the other two to the gate where their plane waited. She checked her watch. Richard had about thirty minutes to get there before their plane took off.

"Will my son get here in time?" Mrs. Anderson asked, her voice trembling.

"Yes, I'm sure he will. He seems to be very efficient."

"Oh, yes, he is."

Molly's words seemed to have settled down Toby's grandmother. She relaxed in her seat, but Molly suspected if Richard didn't get there quickly, she would start worrying all over again.

Toby leaned in against Molly. "Is he going to go with us?"

"Yes, Toby, he is."

Mrs. Anderson looked at Toby. "How old are you?"

Molly stared at her, her mouth agape. Toby seemed to be taken aback, too. His grandmother didn't know how old he was?

"I'm eight," Toby finally said.

"Oh, you were born a year after your mother married."

Toby looked at her curiously. "Did you know my mommy?"

The woman suddenly burst into tears.

For the first time since she met him, Molly discovered a desire for Richard's presence.

CHAPTER TWO

MOLLY discovered her desire for Richard's arrival wasn't a good thing.

"What have you done to my mother?" he demanded roughly as soon as he reached them.

"I didn't do anything to your mother. Toby asked an innocent question, that's all."

She regretted that comment, too, because the man immediately turned to glare at the boy.

When they announced the boarding of the first-class passengers, Molly immediately stood and returned Mrs. Anderson's ticket to her son. "Toby and I will go ahead and board."

After they were seated on the plane, Toby by the window, he leaned over and asked in a whisper, "Did I make her cry?"

"Not really, sweetie. I guess she's still emotional about your mommy. After all, your mommy was her little girl."

"Oh."

Toby tensed and Molly looked up to see Richard and his mother entering the plane. Their seats, it appeared, were across the aisle from her and Toby.

Richard nodded in her direction, but she said nothing.

Perhaps he would continue to blame her for his mother's tears. She didn't know, but she didn't see how she could be expected to have realized Toby's question would've brought that intense reaction.

There was no more conversation between them. Toby, much to Molly's relief, fell asleep after the first hour. Molly pulled out a novel she'd been reading and passed the time that way. When the pilot announced their approach to the airport, she woke Toby.

"The plane is landing. Don't you want to see where you're going to live?"

"Can you see it from the airplane?" Toby asked in surprise.

Molly chuckled. She'd already discovered Toby was very literal. "No, honey, I just meant you could see the area. You'll see your new home later."

"I miss my old home," Toby said sadly.

Molly hugged him to her, as much as the seat belts allowed. "I know you do. But you'll like this one, too, I'm sure." She hoped she wasn't lying.

"Okay," Toby whispered.

She held his hand while the plane landed and then taxied to the gate. Since he'd brought nothing on board with him, they were ready to exit the plane at once. When Richard indicated they should go ahead, Molly led Toby off the plane and to their baggage claim. She was sure the Andersons were right behind them, but she didn't turn to look for them, not wanting to give Richard that satisfaction.

Then that deep voice came over her shoulder. "If you'll point out your bags, Molly, I'll get them off the carousel."

"Thank you. They haven't come by yet."

When she saw her bags, along with Toby's, she pointed them out. A skycap loaded them on his pushcart.

"Molly, will you keep an eye on Toby and my mother while I go get my car?"

She heard the words not said. "And please don't make my mother cry."

"Yes, of course," she replied.

Molly led them to a bench where they could sit until Richard arrived with the car.

Much to her surprise, he pulled up in a medium-size SUV and got out, opening the back for the luggage. She had assumed he'd drive a Mercedes or a Lexus, since he was supposed to be rich. After she got Mrs. Anderson and Toby settled, she followed him into the back seat.

"Thank you for getting them loaded," Richard said as he slid behind the wheel.

"Thank you for loading the luggage." It seemed the only polite thing to say in response to his remark. Had he thought she'd remain standing on the sidewalk, unable to move without his guidance?

He flashed her a look in the rearview mirror. She smiled, determined to let him know she wasn't bothered by his attitude.

She turned her attention to the sights outside her window, pointing out interesting things to Toby.

"Where's the ocean?" Toby whispered.

"Um, I don't think there is an ocean nearby, Toby."

Toby appeared startled. "They don't have an ocean?"

"Actually, we do," Richard said over his shoulder, "but it's on the southern part of the state, which is about five or six hours away."

"Oh," Toby said softly.

"Did you go to the ocean a lot?" his uncle asked.

"Yes, with Mommy," Toby said.

"Susan always liked the ocean," Mrs. Anderson said, surprising everyone.

"Yes, Mom, she did."

No one spoke after that exchange.

When they got off the freeway, they turned into a neighborhood with large houses and big trees. The house whose driveway they pulled into was the biggest of them all. Both Molly and Toby stared at it in surprise.

Richard looked over his shoulder. "You can get out now. We're home."

Toby turned to look at Molly, panic on his face.

Molly squeezed his hand. "It's all right," she whispered, but she wasn't sure she believed it herself. The house was huge, but the stone façade made it look cold and unwelcoming. The air, too, was cold and windy, furthering the impression.

Molly was going to have to buy a coat. Good thing she was earning a lot of money on this job.

Pasting a smile on her face, she said, "Come on, Toby. It'll be fun. We can explore."

She helped the little boy out of the vehicle and shivered as a cold wind blew.

"Hurry inside so you'll be warm," Richard said.

Since they parked in the driveway beside the side entrance, Molly assumed he meant that door. She opened the door and led Toby inside. They were standing in a small entryway next to the kitchen.

Suddenly there was a flurry of movement as three

people rushed forward. Toby pressed against Molly, but the male and two female strangers passed them by and greeted the Andersons.

The younger woman took Mrs. Anderson by the arm and led her away. The man, tall and wiry, was sent to the vehicle to bring in the luggage. Richard consulted with the other woman.

Molly and Toby stood there, not sure what they were supposed to do.

Richard stepped toward them. "I'll show you your rooms if you'll follow me."

Molly nodded and followed him, Toby clinging tightly to her hand. No wonder. He had sounded as remote as a hotel employee. They went up a grand stairway to the second floor. He turned left and led them down the hall to two rooms side by side.

"These rooms are actually connected by a door inside. I thought you might want to leave the door open the first few nights Toby is here, Molly, if you don't mind."

"No, I don't. That's a good idea, right, Toby?"

Richard opened a door. "This will be your room, Toby."

Molly walked into the room with the little boy. "This is great, isn't it, Toby? You have a lot of windows and you can look at the garden behind the house. When it's warmer, you may be able to play there."

The man nodded. "Of course." Then he crossed to another door and opened it. "This will be your room, Molly."

It was beautiful, not what she expected. She laughed to herself as she realized nannies were housed in the attic only in gothic novels.

"Thank you, it's lovely, Richard."

He frowned, as if she'd said something wrong. What could it have been? She'd smiled at him, trying to be gracious.

"Yes, well, I need to see about my mother. If you need anything, please ask Delores or Louisa. They'll be glad to help you."

So they'd already been handed off to the staff. Molly nodded in response, but she didn't say anything. If she'd spoken, she might've said the wrong thing. The man had been kind to Toby when he'd shown him the room, but it was clear he was going about his business as usual.

One thing was certain: Richard Anderson did not have a kind heart.

One thing was certain: Richard was irritated with Molly. Condemnation fairly glowed in her green eyes. He had a lot of things on his plate. He'd brought her here to help Toby settle in okay. That was her job. And he wasn't going to be chastised for doing his job by someone he'd hired.

He shook his head as he went to the other end of the house where his mother's suite was located. Tapping lightly on the door, he stood waiting for it to open.

Louisa came to the door.

"I'd like to see my mother. Is she asleep?" he asked.

"No, sir." Louisa stepped aside and swung the door wide. Then she silently made her way out.

Richard took the chair opposite his mother, in a sitting room professionally done in southwestern decor. He noticed she looked tired, drawn, much the same as she'd looked for the past year and a half. The depression had taken its toll on her. And now, the funeral.

Before he could speak, she said, "You know, Richard,

ever since the incident between Susan and your father, I've regretted her leaving. But never like I regret it now." She looked up and there were tears in her eyes. "She ran away because of your father—but I had nine years to make it right and never did. I was too afraid to cross him." The tears spilled down her cheeks now as she said, "And after he died, I was too distraught and depressed to make the move. I thought I had more time…"

Richard reached out and took her hands in his, rubbing the tops of her hands with his thumb. Her skin was soft and firm, and he realized as he looked at her just how lovely a woman she was. Elizabeth Anderson had once been in the Dallas social scene, a benefactor, an organizer, a supporter of the arts. She had a closet full of designer gowns and suits for the variety of functions she'd attended and chaired. But in the last eighteen months she'd spent most of her time right here in this room. Had he done enough to help her through her hard time?

He could certainly help now.

"You know, Mom, the incident had nothing to do with you." Funny, he thought, how they referred to it—"the incident." As if giving it a generic name made it more ephemeral, less real. But the day Susan walked out couldn't have been more real. He remembered it as if it were yesterday, though it was almost a decade ago. It was the day everything changed.

Susan and their father, James, had always butted heads. He was an autocrat and Susan a free spirit—a doomed combination. When James laid down a law, he expected it enacted, but his sister had a hard time conforming; she was confident and eager and resented her father's strict hand. But that didn't deter James. He tried to control everything:

her clothes, her friends, her studies. But the day he'd tried
to control her heart was the end. He'd found out she was
seeing a young man behind his back, a young man from a
working-class family who was studying to become a
teacher. Kevin Astin was far from the rich, privileged, connected man James had wanted for Susan. He gave her an
ultimatum: ditch him or get out.

Susan opted for the latter. In an hour she'd packed her
bags and left Highland Park for good. In nine years she
hadn't ever been back.

She moved to Florida with Kevin, whom she married
almost immediately. And a year later they had Toby. The
nephew Richard had never seen until yesterday.

In the intervening years he'd spoken to Susan twice, and
his mother never, both fearful of James Anderson's wrath. Not
that he'd ever been physical with them; but his disapproval
took other forms, equally distasteful. Somehow it had just
seemed easier to agree with him, or at least conform to him.

Richard realized he was equally to blame. Nothing, no one,
should have kept him from his sister, kept Elizabeth from her
daughter. But there was nothing either of them could do now,
except pray for forgiveness. And care for Toby.

He told his mother all that, and she listened to him.
After a while her tears stopped, her sobs turned into steady,
even breathing. She held his hand and almost mystically
he could feel her pain exiting. He knew nothing could ever
erase the agony she'd suffered, but Elizabeth was on the
way to recovery.

They talked about Susan, about what they remembered,
about what they'd heard of her recent life at the funeral.
Richard realized this felt more like a funeral than what

they'd endured in Florida. This was a memorial to Susan Anderson Astin, who would live forever in their hearts, where she belonged.

Elizabeth smiled faintly. "I don't know what I'd do without you, Richard. But I do know what I intend to do." She stood up and looked around. "I intend to get out of the prison I've made of this room and start living again. The way Susan would want me to. And I intend to care for her son."

"That's the Elizabeth Anderson I know." Richard hugged her and she held him tight, conveying her gratitude in the maternal embrace.

"Now, Mom, I have to get to the office. I'll try my best to get home in time for dinner." For the first time in over a year, when he closed her bedroom door he knew his mother would be okay.

And so would he.

He walked back downstairs to the kitchen, where their cook, Delores, ruled. Now nearing fifty, the Mexican-American woman had worked for the Andersons for decades, as had her husband, Albert.

"Delores, I'm going to the office for a couple of hours. If the nurse or the child needs anything, please take care of them."

"Yes, sir, Richard."

Richard's law firm was located downtown, very close to their neighborhood, Highland Park, an exclusive area. It only took a few minutes to reach the parking garage connected to the building where the law firm had offices.

As expected, he found a pile of messages and mail on his desk that his secretary had sorted and opened for him. After dealing with those matters, he asked his secretary to gather the partners in his office for a quick briefing. Then there was a list of phone calls to be returned. By the time he'd finished half the calls, he put aside the rest of them for the morning and packed up to go home.

He'd probably already missed dinner. Normally he made it home for dinner at least three nights a week, or else his mother ate her meal upstairs in her suite.

Tonight, when he got home, he found the dinner table set for four. "No one's eaten yet?" he asked Delores as he came in.

"Your mother requested we wait for you."

"The boy didn't get too hungry?"

"No, sir. I gave Toby and Molly a snack about five."

"Thanks, Delores. Please call them down to dinner."

He carried his briefcase to his office, stepped into the connecting bath and washed his hands. Then he came back to the dining room.

Molly and Toby were standing there, seemingly unsure of where they should sit.

"Good evening. I hope your afternoon was relaxing?"

Molly nudged the boy. He said, "Yes, sir."

"Good, Toby. And you, Molly? Did you have a pleasant afternoon?" He was determined to show no prejudice to her.

"Yes, I did, Richard, thank you. We're all unpacked and we've familiarized ourselves with the house and your staff. They're all very nice."

"Yes, we're most fortunate," Richard said with a smile. "But it doesn't sound like your afternoon was very restful."

Molly raised her gaze to his. "Neither of us needed rest. Toby was curious about his new home. Albert even gave us a tour of the backyard after we unpacked."

"Weren't you cold? I noticed you didn't wear a coat on the trip."

"No, neither of us has a coat because it didn't get that cold in Florida. But Albert promised to drive us to a store to buy coats tomorrow."

"Good. I'll be glad to pay for them."

"If you insist, you can pay for Toby's. I'll pay for mine."

Richard frowned. He wasn't used to such resistance.

"Richard?" His mother stood at the door of the dining room.

He crossed over to take her hand and lead her to the table after kissing her cheek. "Hello, Mother. It was kind of you to wait for me to get home."

"I wanted our first meal to be a family one," Elizabeth Anderson said.

"Then let's all sit down," he suggested. He showed his mother to the seat at the head of the table. He indicated Toby and Molly should take the two seats to her left. As they did so, he sat in the chair to his mother's right.

Once they were seated, Elizabeth rang the small bell sitting beside her plate. Almost immediately, the kitchen door opened and Louisa entered with a tray. She carefully set a bowl of soup in front of each of them.

Toby leaned over to Molly and whispered, "What is this?"

Richard, hiding a grin, said, "It's broccoli cheese soup, Toby, one of my mother's favorites." He was feeling relieved that things were going so well. He'd gone to the office and his mother had rested, and the nurse had taken care of the boy, as he'd planned.

"Oh. Uh, it looks good."

"Very nice manners, Toby. Your mother would be proud

of you," Richard said softly. He didn't want to upset his mother, but Susan deserved her due.

Instead of bursting into tears as she normally would have done upon mention of Susan, his mother smiled faintly. Their talk had indeed helped her. "Yes, I believe she did a good job teaching Toby proper behavior."

"I agree, Mrs. Anderson," Molly chimed in. "I can't wait to try the soup. I haven't gotten used to this cold weather yet."

Richard laughed. "It doesn't get that cold here, Molly. Now in Colorado, this would be late spring weather."

"Where is Colorado?" Toby asked.

"It's a state north of here where a lot of Texans go to ski."

"Water-ski?" Toby asked.

"No, Toby, snow skiing."

"With real snow? I've never seen snow, except on TV," the boy confessed.

"Maybe after you get your casts off, we can fly to Colorado and try some snow skiing," Richard suggested.

"I'd like that!" Toby said in excitement. "Would you like that, Molly?"

"I'm sure it would be fun, Toby, but I'll probably be back at work by then."

Richard watched the enthusiasm fade from the little boy's face.

"But you could send me pictures of you skiing. That would be wonderful. You might even build a snowman for me."

"Could we do that?" Toby asked, looking at Richard.

"Sure, Toby, we could do that."

"Right now, though, you need to eat your soup before it gets cold," Molly said with a smile.

Richard watched her. While some people would have been overwhelmed by the quick transition, the gamut of emotions and personalities, Molly kept her composure. And she was wonderful with Toby. Now she not only offered a way for Toby to share his excitement with her, but she'd reminded him of his behavior.

The boy at once picked up his spoon and tried the soup. Then he looked at his grandmother. "The soup is very good."

"Yes, it is, isn't it? We'll have to tell Delores what a good job she's done," Elizabeth said, smiling at Toby.

"Am I supposed to call you Grandma?" Toby asked.

"Yes, I think that's what you should call me. Do you mind?" Elizabeth asked with more energy than she'd shown in months.

Richard stared at his mother. She looked better already, a gleam in her blue eyes he hadn't seen in a long time. He knew it would take time for her to regain her old self, but she was on her way. After all, she'd barely recovered from his father's death eighteen months ago, when she'd learned of Susan's death. Somehow, when he'd expected her to give up on life, she seemed to have found a new lease on it. Still, he'd have to keep a close watch on her to make sure she didn't overdo it.

When they finished their soup, Elizabeth rang her bell again and Louisa came in to remove their bowls. Albert followed with a large serving tray.

Richard drew in a deep breath of roast beef perfectly cooked with attending vegetables. He smiled at Louisa. It was his favorite meal. "Thank Delores for me, Louisa."

"Yes, sir," Louisa said with a grin.

They were all enjoying their meal when Toby asked a question that got their attention. "Don't you have a Christmas tree?"

Elizabeth assured him they did. It was in the living room.

"But I didn't see it today."

"You may have missed the living room, dear. It's the room by the front door. Some people call it a parlor."

"I don't think we went in that room, Toby," Molly said softly.

"You would remember it if you saw it, Toby," Elizabeth continued. "It's silver with gold balls on it. It's quite striking."

"No, Grandma, Christmas trees are green, not silver."

"Toby, some trees aren't real," Molly hurriedly explained. "They're made out of other things."

Toby looked puzzled. "Why?"

Molly looked at Richard, a clear plea for assistance.

"Real trees are messy, Toby. Plus, if you have an artificial tree, you can reuse it every year."

"Is that good, Molly?" Toby asked.

"For some people it is."

"I like green trees," Toby asserted. Then tears glistened in his eyes as he continued, "Me and Mommy and Daddy decorated our tree with all our favorite ornaments."

Molly leaned over and whispered something in Toby's ear and the little boy tried to wipe away the tears.

"Mrs. Anderson," Molly asked, "would there be a room where Toby could have a green tree this year? As a sort of memorial to his parents?"

Richard spoke up. "My mother can't—"

"Yes, I think we could do that," Elizabeth said at the same time.

"Mother, I don't think you can take on that task. It will be too much for you."

"It wouldn't be, Richard, if you'd help."

The other two were sitting quietly, watching the conversation between him and his mother. Richard almost groaned aloud. He had too much to do as it was. But he could tell his mother wanted to make the effort for her grandson.

"All right, Mother. In what room would you like to put the green tree?"

"I think my sitting room would do. Then we could enjoy it all day long."

"Of course you could, if you want an eight-year-old running in and out."

Molly spoke up. "Toby and I came across a garden room with a tiled floor and some pretty durable furniture in it. Wouldn't that be a good room for a real tree, so the pine needles won't stick in the carpet?" She looked at Richard.

"We don't use that room often in the winter. Do you think that would be a good idea, Richard?" Elizabeth asked her son.

"I'm sure it would be fine, Mom. Albert can take Molly and Toby out to find a tree tomorrow, if they want."

Toby frowned. "But the daddy always comes to carry the tree and tie it on the roof of the car."

Richard smiled. "We don't have a daddy here, Toby. I promise Albert can carry the tree for you. He's very strong."

"No, I think Toby is right," Elizabeth spoke with more authority than Richard had heard from her since he was a small boy himself.

"Right about what, Mom?" he asked.

"I think we should go as a family. That's what we did when you were a little boy. When you get home tomorrow evening, we'll go find a tree." She nodded, as if to punctuate her statement.

"I'm not sure when I'll be able to get home, Mom. I missed two days of work."

"Richard, I don't think you should miss buying the tree. This will be Toby's first Christmas with us. It's important."

Richard sighed, thinking of all the work he had piled up for him when he got to the office in the morning. And now he'd have to get home at a decent hour tomorrow night to go buy a blasted Christmas tree!

"And when will the presents get here?" Toby asked.

"Why, I suppose Santa will bring them Christmas Day," Elizabeth assured him with a smile.

"No, I mean the presents that were under our tree at home." Toby turned to Molly. "They will come, won't they?"

"I don't know, honey. I'm sure they'll get here sometime, but it might not be before Christmas."

"But they have to! I think Mommy wrapped up my puppy!"

CHAPTER THREE

ALL three adults stared at the little boy.

"What?" Molly asked, not sure she'd heard correctly.

"Oh, no!" Elizabeth said, covering her mouth with her hand.

Richard drew a deep breath. "Toby, I don't think that would've been possible. Puppies can't live in a closed-up box."

Once again tears formed in Toby's eyes. "But my mommy promised me a puppy for Christmas!"

Molly automatically put her arm around Toby. "Richard isn't saying your mommy wasn't getting you a puppy. He's just saying it wasn't wrapped up. She'd probably made arrangements for picking up the puppy on Christmas Eve."

"So I'll still get my puppy?"

Molly looked at Richard. She figured he should be the one to answer that question. She couldn't imagine a dog in their elegant home.

"Uh, no, I don't think so. We don't know where she'd purchased a dog."

Toby slumped back in his chair, devastation on his face.

Molly squeezed his shoulder and said softly, "Finish your dinner like a big boy, Toby."

He sat up straighter and looked at Molly for approval. She managed a smile for him, hoping he wouldn't realize how much she sympathized with him. It would only make him weaker.

"I'm sure Santa will bring you some wonderful presents, Toby," Elizabeth assured him.

Toby managed a smile for his grandmother.

Elizabeth immediately rang the bell. When Louisa entered, she said, "We're ready for dessert now, Louisa, please."

Richard looked at his mother in surprise. "We are?"

"Yes, I believe Toby has finished his meal and dessert will make him feel better." Again she smiled at Toby, ignoring Richard's half-filled plate.

With a sigh and a regretful look as Louisa collected his plate, Richard said, "Dessert must be good tonight, Toby. We don't always get any dessert."

"Me, neither. But I like dessert," Toby added, again managing a smile for his grandmother.

Molly hid her smile, afraid Richard would guess she was laughing inside about his consternation as his plate was taken from him. But he was being a good sport about it, which earned him marks in her book, in spite of his lack of warmth toward her.

Dessert was chocolate cake with chocolate ice cream—Toby's favorite. Molly ate some of it, but she didn't clean her plate like the two males did.

Elizabeth didn't touch hers, seeming more engrossed in Toby's enjoyment of the dessert.

After dinner was over, Molly suggested Toby tell his relatives good-night and she'd take him up to bed. Since saying good-night at home had included kisses and hugs for his parents, Toby hugged his grandmother, much to her delight, and kissed her cheek. Then he moved on to Richard and did the same.

To Molly's relief, both of them appeared grateful for Toby's nightly ritual. Molly took the boy's hand and led him up the stairs to his room.

"You did really well tonight, Toby," Molly told him as he was preparing for his bath. She'd already run the bathwater as soon as they'd reached his room.

He raised his head to stare at her. "What do you mean?"

"Well, you used good table manners, and you behaved very well when you realized you might not get a dog for Christmas."

"Yeah. I want a puppy so much. But I guess a dog wouldn't do so well in this big house. He might get lost."

"Yes, he might. After you have a bath, I'll read you a story," Molly said, trying to recall the books she'd packed. "I don't know which books I packed. Is there one you want me to read?"

"Any of the Berenstain Bear books. They're a lot of fun. And I can read them myself."

"Ah. Good. Then I'll let you read one to me tonight. And I might buy a copy of *Charlotte's Web*. Have you ever read that book?"

"No, but my mommy was going to read it to me if Santa brought me it."

"Okay. Well, tonight, we'll stick to the Berenstain Bears. Go hop in and take your bath. I'll go see if your uncle will loan you a T-shirt for the night. We should be able to get one of his over your casts."

"Do you think he'll mind?" Toby asked hesitantly.

"Why do you ask that?" She was afraid her attitude toward Richard might have been passed on to Toby without her realizing it.

"He—he scares me a little bit."

"I think that's just because you don't know him well yet. I'll be right back." Molly smiled at Toby and left his room. She didn't know how to avoid speaking to Richard. She wished she did. But she couldn't make a big deal about it. Otherwise, she might think about him like Toby did. As the enemy.

She ran downstairs, but she didn't find Richard in the dining room. She went into the kitchen and asked Louisa if she knew where Richard had gone.

"Yes, ma'am," said the Mexican woman about her own age. "He went upstairs to his room."

She got directions from Louisa and ran back up the stairs, turning to the right until she reached the bedroom opposite Elizabeth's. She tapped softly on the door and waited. But she couldn't shake the feeling that she was like Daniel about to enter the lion's den.

Richard settled in a comfortable chair in front of his fireplace, warmed by the fire. He had some legal reading to catch up on.

But his mind was filled with the evening he'd just spent downstairs. There was no question that Toby's arrival had changed the dynamics of the household. He was rethinking his plan of turning the little boy over to his nurse and continuing on with his life. After all, he had just about completed his reworking of his father's law firm. Instead of personal injury cases, he had changed the focus to corporate law.

He thought he'd finally be able to return to the pleasant life he'd always led. For the past eighteen months, he'd dealt with the law firm and with his mother. While he and his father had not agreed in many things, he had truly mourned his death. And feared he'd soon lose his mother. Tonight, as she'd focused all her attention on Toby, she appeared to have grown younger before Richard's very eyes.

He wondered if Molly had come to that same conclusion. He'd noticed how closely she'd watched his mother. It would be nice to be able to talk to her about his mother. After all, she was a nurse.

He shouldn't be thinking about Molly as a friend. He was paying her salary. That would be like asking Delores for advice. Of course, he'd done that. After all, Delores had been with them for more than twenty years. And Molly didn't look anything like the plump, dark-haired Delores, either. He immediately shut that thought away.

But thoughts of Molly persisted in spite of his efforts to concentrate on other things. Her hair had glinted in the light from the chandelier in the dining room, sparking more red tonight than he'd noticed before. Concern had filled her green eyes when Toby had made his statement about the puppy he was expecting. Richard had been tempted to laugh until he'd seen Molly's reaction.

With a sigh, he tried again to put away all thoughts of Molly. As beautiful as she was, she had no place in his life.

Unfortunately, for the last eighteen months no woman had had a place in his life, except his mother.

Prior to his father's death, he'd enjoyed a nice social life. However, with his father's death had come the opportunity to change the law firm's focus, which demanded most of his time. His mother had demanded the rest of it.

That was the problem, he realized. He was thinking of Molly because he missed…he missed having a woman in his life.

Just as he managed to focus on his reading, he heard a knock. With a frown, he rose and went to the door. Delores or Albert must have a problem. Normally they didn't disturb him after he'd gone upstairs.

Swinging open the door, he discovered his caller to be the woman he'd had on his mind. He could only think of one reason she would be there, and it wasn't one he was willing to cooperate with. At least not here.

"Molly?" he said, frowning at her.

"I'm sorry to disturb you, Richard, but I have a favor to ask."

"I don't think I'll be willing to grant that favor, Molly. It would be rather improper with my mother across the hall."

Her green eyes widened in shock as she took in his meaning, which made him realize he'd made a mistake.

"What do you want?" he asked, hoping she'd forget what he'd implied.

"I wanted to borrow a T-shirt from you for Toby. I'll buy him a couple tomorrow, but his shirts are too small to fit comfortably over his casts."

Her stiffened demeanor told him she hadn't forgiven him for the beginning of their conversation.

"Yes, of course, I'll get one for you," he said, leaving the door open. As he crossed the room to open a drawer, he tried to figure out how to apologize for his initial words without admitting what he'd actually thought. Or how his pulse had raced.

When he got back to the door, a white T-shirt in his hand, he said, "I'm sorry I, uh, reacted in the, uh, wrong way." He thought he sounded like a teenager speaking to a teacher.

"I can assure you I won't bother you in the evenings again, Richard."

Her words were cool, distant, and told him his apology hadn't gotten him very far.

"I'm glad to be of assistance, Molly."

She took the T-shirt from him and walked away with a muttered thanks. He watched her until she entered Toby's bedroom.

Damn, he'd messed up big time. He'd have to make it up to Molly tomorrow.

But how?

Molly and Toby came to breakfast after Richard had left for work. Elizabeth came down just a couple of minutes after them and they all enjoyed breakfast in a small room off the kitchen. It was a cozy room to eat in, and both Molly and Toby were more relaxed.

"Mrs. Anderson, can—"

"Please, dear, you must call me Elizabeth."

"Oh, thank you, Elizabeth. I wanted to ask if Albert could take me and Toby to a store to buy coats this morning, and maybe to a Christmas store to buy some ornaments for the tree?"

"Of course he can, and I'll go with you. Richard gave me strict instructions to pay for all your purchases today."

"Oh, surely not all of them. I'll pay for my own coat and anything else I buy for myself."

"He was quite clear in his instructions."

"Well, we'll see. Not having bought a coat before, I'm not sure what they cost."

"Are you thinking about a fur coat?" Elizabeth asked.

Molly stared at her. "Fur? Oh, no, not at all!"

"But a fur coat will last longer than a cloth coat. I've had a mink coat my husband bought me thirty years ago, and it still looks good even now."

Molly smiled. "But I'm going back to Florida. I wouldn't have any use for a fur coat. Nor could I afford it. I thought we'd go to Target and find reasonably priced coats."

"I usually go to Neiman's for clothes."

"I don't think Neiman's would have what we need, Elizabeth, but you don't have to accompany us. We'll be fine."

"Oh, but I want to go with you. It'll be fun. Richard left you a note to explain everything. I put it in the pocket of my robe so I wouldn't forget it. Here it is."

Molly unfolded the note. In it, Richard assured her, as his mother had done, that they would pay for whatever she wanted. He also cautioned her not to let his mother get too tired.

She could definitely follow that caution, but Molly didn't think she could let him pay for all her purchases if they were for her. She'd find a way around that order.

"Well, if you're going with us, plan on leaving at ten. Isn't that when the stores open?"

"I believe so," Elizabeth said. "That gives us almost an hour to get ready."

Molly smiled in agreement, though she didn't think an hour would be necessary for either Toby or herself.

When they met downstairs at the assigned time, Elizabeth was dressed in a chic wool suit that shouted designer. Molly was in slacks with a cotton sweater. They were the warmest clothes she owned. Toby was in jeans and a knit shirt that would fit over his casts.

"Albert promised to have the car warmed up so you two wouldn't freeze to death before we can get you coats."

"I'll have to thank him," Molly said, turning to the garage.

Elizabeth redirected her out the front door. "Albert has pulled the car around."

As Elizabeth had said, the car was warm and they barely felt the north wind that chilled the air. All three of them sat in the back seat while Albert drove the car.

When they reached Target, Albert let them out at the front door and promised to wait in the parking lot for them.

"This makes shopping easy, doesn't it?" Molly commented.

"Yes, it does. Albert is a dear." Elizabeth took Toby's hand. "You must hold my hand, Toby, so we won't get lost."

"Yes, Grandma. I won't let you get lost."

Molly wasn't sure who was protecting whom, but that was okay with her. They went to the children's department first and found a ski-jacket for Toby. They bought it a little large to fit over his casts. Elizabeth added some sweaters and long sleeve polo shirts to the pile, too. Then they went to the men's department to buy him some large T-shirts.

Molly explained to Elizabeth about them borrowing one of Richard's the night before.

"Then we should get at least four T-shirts," Elizabeth said. She put that many in their basket. When they reached the women's department, Elizabeth thought Molly should buy a good wool coat that would last for many years. Molly didn't remind her that she would be returning to Florida in a month.

Since the wool coat was navy and would go with almost anything, Molly was pleased with it. She added a couple of sweaters to the basket for her, too.

"Now, shall we look at the Christmas tree ornaments?" she asked.

"Oh, not here. There's a lovely Christmas store that I've been to before. They have all kinds of specialty ornaments. Let's go there," Elizabeth insisted.

Molly agreed. She managed to convince Elizabeth that she should pay for her purchases.

Albert sped them away to the store Elizabeth had chosen. Inside, everything shimmered and glowed as the ornaments were displayed beautifully. Toby was thrilled, especially when his grandmother told him he should pick all the ornaments. He raced around the store, not wanting to miss anything. But he made very thoughtful choices.

"He reminds me so much of Susan," Elizabeth said softly as she watched him make his selections.

"He is a terrific little boy, but you mustn't spoil him too much," Molly warned. "Susan taught him beautiful manners, and we wouldn't want her teaching to go to waste."

"You're quite right, dear, but as long as you're here with him, I'm sure you will keep him in line," Elizabeth said with a big smile.

Molly thought about reminding Elizabeth that she would be going back to her life in Florida after Christmas, but she didn't bother. Richard would make sure his mother knew that.

They returned home at noon, just in time for a wonderful lunch that Delores had prepared. Then Molly suggested everyone lie down for an hour or two so they'd be rested for the Christmas tree hunt that evening.

While Elizabeth and Toby took their naps, Molly removed the tags from their purchases, including the ornaments, which she carried down to the garden room. They'd bought a tree skirt and some colored lights, too. Toby had also chosen an angel to go on the top of the tree.

He had assured Elizabeth it looked just like the angel that had topped his tree in Florida. Though it was expensive, Elizabeth had declared it the perfect choice for the top of Toby's tree at their house, too.

Molly had enjoyed their shopping as much as the other two. Because she had no family, she usually only decorated a tiny tree that sat on her dining table. She was excited just looking at all the ornaments they'd bought. A big tree, with presents under it, filled her with an anticipation that she hadn't experienced since she was a small child with her parents.

Her parents had died in a car accident, much as Toby's had, but she'd had no relatives to take her in. She'd spent the rest of her childhood in foster homes. None of them had celebrated Christmas as she'd remembered it with her parents.

Now, though she was alone, she tried to make Christmas special for those around her. She'd already purchased Secret Santa presents for the patients in the hospital. Since she'd left early with Toby, she'd left the gifts with another nurse to pass out for Christmas.

She usually did a lot of baking, taking goodies to her friends at the hospital and neighbors in her apartment building. She would miss baking. Unless she could convince Toby to make Christmas cookies with her.

She smiled. She wasn't sure Delores would let them invade her kitchen.

When Toby woke up, Molly kept him busy by playing a game with him. She had a deck of cards with her and together they played more hands of Battle and Go Fish than she could count.

At five o'clock, Louisa knocked on Toby's door. Richard had called to tell them he would be there in half an hour to go find a Christmas tree. Could they please be ready?

"Yes, of course, Louisa. Have you told Mrs. Anderson?"

"Yes, ma'am. She said she would be ready, too."

Molly put the deck of cards away, reminding herself to buy some games the next time she had a chance. Toby was a smart little boy. She didn't want him getting bored. According to Elizabeth, he wouldn't be going to school until after the New Year, since most of the schools in town had ended their semester this week.

Toby could hardly contain his excitement. Molly took the child down early to wait in the garden room and discuss where they thought the tree should be placed.

When Toby finally decided on the corner of the room, she reminded him that Elizabeth and Richard might decide otherwise.

"Yeah, but I think Grandma will agree with me."

"You think so, do you?" Molly asked him with a grin.

"She's nice, isn't she?" he asked, smiling back.

"Yes, she is. You're a lucky little boy."

Toby's blue eyes clouded over. "I'm not lucky 'cause my mommy and daddy died."

Molly hugged him. "I know, sweetie, but the same thing happened to me, and I didn't have a grandma to take me in."

Her revelation caught Toby's attention. "Your mommy and daddy died, too?"

"Yes, when I was seven."

He immediately hugged Molly. "I'm sorry."

"Thank you, Toby, but it was a long time ago. I told you so you could appreciate your grandmother and uncle taking you in. That makes you a lucky boy."

"Did you have to live alone?"

Molly laughed. "No. I might've been better off if I had, but I was put in a foster home."

"What's that?"

With a sigh, Molly said, "It's a family who gets paid to take care of you. Usually they have too many people in the house and they don't have time to make you feel special. Like your grandma." Or even loved. In the two foster homes she'd lived in, they had assigned chores, but they hadn't shown appreciation or love for what she did. She'd almost felt faceless.

"That must've made you sad," Toby said solemnly.

"Yes, it did. But I—" She was interrupted by the sound of a car pulling into the driveway.

Toby rushed out of the room, calling over his shoulder, "I bet that's Richard!"

Molly sighed and followed him more slowly. The last

thing she wanted to show was enthusiasm for Richard's arrival.

Elizabeth was coming down the stairs as Molly reached the hallway.

"Is that Richard?" she asked.

"I believe so. Toby went to see. He's very excited about the tree."

"I am, too, for the first time in years." She reached the hall and took on a wistful look. "You know, we gave up decorating a real tree after the children went to college. It just didn't seem worth the effort without a child to enjoy it."

Molly smiled. "But you do have a Christmas tree in the living room. It's quite beautiful."

"Yes, but it's not the same. Now with Toby, I feel like I've been given a second chance at life. It's invigorating." She returned the smile and grabbed Molly's hand. "Let's go see if it was Richard."

The two ladies went to the side entrance and found Toby telling Richard about all their purchases that day.

"You must've shopped all day!"

"Not quite," Elizabeth said as she and Molly arrived in the doorway.

Richard stared at his mother. "You sound like you went with them. Are you too tired to go out now?"

"Absolutely not!"

Richard frowned as Toby and Elizabeth went out to get in his car. "I thought I warned you not to let Mom overdo it," he said harshly, blocking Molly as she started to go past him.

How dare he accuse her of not doing her job! She'd done as he'd requested—even if it hadn't been part of her employment arrangements. They stood mere inches apart, so close

Molly could feel the cold emanating from his overcoat. But she didn't back up. She raised her chin and looked him square in the eyes. "Did she sound exhausted to you?"

Richard held her gaze a few seconds, as if measuring her resolve. Then, finally, in one swift motion he turned and went out the door. "I'll hold you responsible if she has a breakdown."

CHAPTER FOUR

MOLLY pressed her lips together. She knew she had done all she could to protect Elizabeth. The lady was talking more and taking more interest in her grandson. If Richard thought that was going to damage his mother, well, he was dead wrong.

Molly knew then and there the only way she'd survive this assignment was to avoid the man altogether. That conviction lasted until she got to the car and saw Elizabeth had left the front seat for her—next to Richard.

Elizabeth must have seen her disgruntled expression, because she said, "I'm going to ride back here with Toby so we can discuss the tree he wants to buy."

Richard slanted at look at Molly. "Join me, won't you, Molly?" he said, sarcasm in his voice.

Okay, so he'd seen her reluctance. It didn't matter. She wasn't here for him. "Thanks," she muttered and circled the vehicle to climb in the front passenger seat.

Molly stared straight ahead. After last night, and again just now with Richard, she intended to keep her distance from this man.

"What kind of tree do you want us to buy?" Richard asked his mother.

"One that pleases Toby," she said.

"Do you have any preferences, Molly?" Richard asked.

"Not in regard to trees," she muttered, hoping that would be the end of any conversation.

"Do you always decorate a tree in Florida?" he persisted.

"A small one." She didn't want to talk to him about her life. It had nothing to do with him. He'd probably think her simple life was pitiful, but she'd created a happy life for herself. It hadn't been easy.

"Why?"

That got her attention. She turned to stare at the handsome man. What was wrong with him? "Because I enjoy Christmas, of course. Don't you?"

"Not particularly."

"Is your middle name Scrooge?"

His lips twitched at the corners. "No, not exactly."

"Well, I hope you'll make an effort for Toby."

"I won't need to. My mother seems to have the bit in her teeth. She'll probably hire someone to play Santa since she wants this Christmas to be special for him."

"Good for her."

"What do you want Santa to bring you for Christmas?"

The man was crazy. He didn't enjoy Christmas and yet he asked about Santa? Molly shrugged. "Nothing."

"Aha! So you're not a fan of Christmas, either!"

Molly scowled at him. "I love Christmas! But that doesn't mean I believe in Santa Claus," she added in a lower voice.

"Then why do you love Christmas if you don't expect to get something special?"

Molly shifted in her seat to look at him squarely. "Christmas isn't about getting something. It's about giving. That's the true meaning of Christmas!"

Or couldn't someone as handsome, rich and successful as Richard Anderson understand that?

Richard drove silently the rest of the way to the Christmas tree lot. The nurse had put him in his place.

Maybe he deserved it. He'd lost his enthusiasm for Christmas the last few years. Or maybe his enthusiasm for life. He wasn't certain.

But he sure didn't want to get into a spitting match with Molly. She seemed well-armed and he didn't like to lose.

He pulled to a stop beside the tree lot. "We're here. Mom, be sure you're wrapped up warmly. We're having a cold December this year. Toby, do you have your coat on?"

"Yeah," he called over his shoulder as he grabbed Elizabeth's hand and off they went toward the trees.

Left alone with Molly, he didn't know what to say. "I guess we should go find a tree," he ventured.

Molly nodded and set off after her charge.

"This one looks nice," he heard her say as he walked toward the trio weaving among the evergreens.

"Oh, no, it's much too short," Elizabeth said. "We need a bigger tree because our ceilings are high." She pointed to a tall one. "What about this one, Toby?"

"It's kind of skinny, isn't it, Grandma?"

"Absolutely right. Let's go look at that one over there." The two hurried eagerly in the direction Elizabeth had pointed. But Molly stayed behind, he noticed. He also noticed her shiver.

"Are you cold?" Richard asked, stepping closer to her.

She backed up. "No. I'm just adjusting to the change in the weather."

Richard nodded. He said nothing for another few minutes, just standing there amongst the trees. Finally he turned again to Molly. "Don't you want to go see the other trees?"

"Whatever they choose will be fine."

More silence. Then, after another few minutes, when Elizabeth and Toby were still darting around the lot, where each tree was staked to the ground like a mini forest, Richard was getting irritated.

"Mom, you and Toby need to choose one. It's too cold to remain out much longer."

He shot a look at Molly, expecting to find disapproval on her face, but she didn't look perturbed by his demand.

"Are you frozen, Molly?"

"N-no, I'm f-fine."

"Why didn't you tell me you were cold?" he asked in irritation. Grabbing her arm, he headed back to the SUV.

"What are you doing?" she demanded, resisting.

"I'm going to warm you up."

The look of horror on her face brought some interesting thoughts to Richard, but he hastily shut them out. "I'm going to start the engine and turn on the heater," he explained with a grin.

"O-Oh."

Once he got her in the front seat, he circled the vehicle and got in to start the engine. "Give me your hands," he said.

Molly stared at him again. "Why?"

"I'm going to hold them in mine. You should've bought some good gloves today when you bought your coat."

"I didn't think I'd be outside this long," she muttered. She finally extended her hands to him. He'd removed his gloves and the warmth of his skin began to penetrate hers.

He did nothing, just held her hands in his larger ones. Still, Molly could feel the heat all the way from her head to her toes. Under her coat she felt flushed. Being in this enclosed space, alone with Richard, was an amazingly intimate exchange with a man she didn't even like two days ago.

Too intimate.

She pulled her hands free. "I think they're warm enough now, thank you."

"Are you sure?" he asked, staring at her.

She felt her cheeks heat and she knew she had to have some distance. "Yes, thank you." She looked over her shoulder. "How—how is the tree search going?"

After telling her to stay inside so she'd be warm, he added, "I'll be back in a minute."

Then he located the two tree-hunters. "Molly is half-frozen. You've got to make a decision."

"We have, Richard. We just decided on this one," Elizabeth said, pointing to a nine-foot Douglas fir.

"Fine, go get in the car and I'll buy it."

"We need to stay here until you get the man's attention. You might buy the wrong tree."

Richard glared at his mother. What had happened to the gentle, indecisive lady he'd lived with for the past eighteen months? "Fine, Mom, I'll be right back."

He went back to the hut where the operators stood around a glowing fire in a half drum. Quickly indicating he was ready to buy his tree, he led one of the men to his mother's side. "This is the tree we want to buy."

"Well, now, you picked a fine one!" the man said with enthusiasm, which in Richard's experience meant that they'd picked an expensive one.

"Mom, take Toby back to the car so he won't catch cold," Richard urged. He handed his credit card to the man to move the process along.

Elizabeth and an excited Toby hurried to the car.

Ten minutes later, Richard had the tree strapped to the top of the SUV and they were on their way.

That was when Toby barraged him with questions, volleying one after the other.

"Did you see the tree?" the boy asked. "Isn't it great?"

"Yes," Richard replied. "You picked a nice one."

"Is it tied on good?"

"Trust me, it's not going anywhere."

"Will we be able to get it down?"

"Albert will help me." Richard couldn't stop smiling at his nephew's enthusiasm. He turned the tables and asked a question. "Do you think you bought enough ornaments for such a big tree?"

"We bought lots. Grandma told me we'd need that many."

"I wanted to be prepared," Elizabeth said.

"Yes, Mom, that was good thinking. I wouldn't want to have to shop for ornaments now. I'm hungry."

"Me, too!" Toby called. "I didn't get a snack today."

"I'm sorry. I'll have to speak to Delores about that," Richard said.

That remark brought Molly to life. "There's no need to speak to Delores. It's my fault we didn't have a snack."

"Why is it your fault?"

"I didn't ask for it. I forgot."

"I see."

He noted her anxious expression. Apparently he hadn't convinced her he wouldn't chew Delores out. The fact that he had never done such a thing hadn't occurred to her.

Elizabeth leaned forward. "Molly, don't worry. He's never said a harsh word to Delores. She might burn the next roast she cooks and that's his favorite meal."

Molly glared at him. "Oh, thank you, Elizabeth."

Richard grinned at her and she looked away.

Obviously Molly wasn't a forgiving woman. At least not to him. He figured Toby was easily forgiven. Even his mother seemed to be in Molly's good graces.

When they reached home, he sent the other three into the house and asked his mother to send Albert out. Together they'd unload the tree and put it right into the stand he'd purchased. They could take it right into the garden room.

A few minutes later, after the tree was standing tall in the garden room, water in its basin, he removed his overcoat and gloves and entered the dining room. It appeared the others were waiting for his arrival.

"I'm sorry to keep you waiting," he said as he entered.

"We had a cup of hot chocolate while we were waiting," his mother said. She rang the bell to let Delores know they were ready.

Dinner began with tortilla soup. Toby seemed even more skeptical this evening, but Molly encouraged him to give it a try.

"It's okay," Toby said with a shrug.

"It will warm you up faster than last night's soup," Richard said. "It's a little spicier."

"It's delicious, Toby," Molly said with a smile.

So the nurse had a stomach for Mexican food? "Have you had tortilla soup before, Molly?"

"Yes, of course. Florida has many Mexican restaurants."

"Oh, really? I would have expected Cuban restaurants, but not Mexican."

"They have both," she answered briefly and continued to eat her soup.

"How does the tree look?" Toby asked.

"Tall. It almost touches the ceiling."

"Do you have a ladder? We'll need one to put the angel on top."

"Yes, I have a ladder," Richard said, sighing, "but you may be too small to climb to the top."

"Richard!" Elizabeth protested.

"That's okay," Toby said calmly. "That's the daddy's job, anyway."

Richard smiled at the little boy. "You know, Toby, I may have to get a list of the daddy jobs. I'm not sure I know all of them."

"It's okay, Uncle Richard. I'll help you."

Uncle Richard?

He couldn't stop the smile that lit his face. This was the first time Toby had called him that. The first time anyone had ever called him that. He knew enough to not make a big deal about it and embarrass Toby, but he liked it. A lot.

Molly, however, leaned over to the boy and said, "You don't really have to make a list. He's just teasing you."

"No, I wasn't, Molly. Not having been a daddy, I don't know all the jobs a dad must do." He certainly hadn't learned the list from his father. The man hadn't spent a lot of time with his family, and when he did, he tended to control them, not be a role model for them. His mother had done the best she could for both him and Susan under the circumstances.

Molly gave him a quick, disbelieving look and turned her attention back to her soup.

"Richard, do you think we can decorate the tree this evening?" Elizabeth asked.

"No, Mom, it's already eight o'clock and Toby will need to go to bed after dinner. Besides, the limbs will look better in the morning. The man at the lot told me they had just put that tree up today."

"Right. Yes, we'll wait until tomorrow to decorate it. But you'll need to be here."

"Tomorrow's the last day before Christmas vacation, Mom. We close at noon."

"Oh, that's right. I'm so glad."

Molly stared at him. "You close tomorrow for Christmas?"

Elizabeth answered her. "It's a trend in Dallas. A lot of businesses close for the two weeks including Christmas and New Year's because so little work gets done. It's mostly parties."

"I see. But it's still a week and a half until Christmas."

"I decided to close tomorrow because it's Friday. Already work has slowed down, so there's not much point in holding everyone there when they want to go shopping and to parties."

"Ah. So you're not taking the vacation out of the goodness of your heart?" Molly asked.

Elizabeth rushed to his defense. "Yes, Molly, he is. His father never let his people have even one day off. They worked all the way through the holidays except for Christmas Day and New Year's Day."

Molly smiled at her hostess. "Of course, Elizabeth, it is generous of Richard."

Richard noticed he didn't get a share of her smile. Which meant, of course, that she didn't really believe he was being generous. Not that he could blame her after his remarks in the car earlier.

When dinner was done, Molly led a sleepy Toby up to his bed, after the good-night hugs and kisses he gave both Richard and his mother.

Elizabeth looked at her son once the other two were gone. "What did you say to Molly earlier about Christmas?"

"What do you mean?"

"I noticed you two talking in the front of the car when we were on our way to the tree lot. She got upset. Which, I think, led to that comment about your generosity."

"I told her I wasn't excited about Christmas."

"I was afraid of that. Don't you think it had something to do with your dad's death and then Susan's?"

Richard sighed. "I don't know, Mom. Christmas hasn't been very exciting since I was still a boy. There's a lot of rushing around and drinking and partying, but it seems kind of empty to me."

"I don't intend to go to many of the society parties this season, and I recommend you don't, either. I feel I have a second chance to make a life for Toby. I know I failed both you and Susan because I wasn't strong enough to stand up to your father. After his death, I was too despondent to make reparations. But Toby needs me now. And he needs you."

"I know, Mom. And I'll try to remember that I'm as close to a daddy as he's going to get now."

"I want to find things to do with Toby. Could you drive us around to see the Christmas lights one night?"

"Of course. Or if it's not too cold, we could take one of the horse and buggy rides around Highland Park."

"That's a wonderful idea, Richard."

"Do you think Toby would enjoy seeing *A Christmas Carol?* Or do you think he'd be afraid of Scrooge?" He could just imagine Molly's reaction to his suggestion.

"I think he'd love it. Are they doing that at the Theater Center?"

"Yes, I think so."

"Wait! I need to get a pen and paper so I can make a list. Then tomorrow I'll discover times and dates and can buy the tickets."

She rushed away from the table. Richard was surprised to find some enthusiasm growing in him for the holiday traditions. It helped that his mother was excited about them.

When she got back to the table, she wrote down his suggestions. He added a few more and decided Toby would be bored once Christmas passed.

"These are wonderful suggestions, Richard, and Toby will love them. He's such a wonderful little boy…and he reminds me so much of Susan."

"Yes, he does, doesn't he? She always demanded the

biggest Christmas tree, too." Richard couldn't hold back a smile, thinking of his little sister.

"Yes," Elizabeth said with a sigh.

"But, Mom, you're not used to all this running around. You have to be sure you don't overdo it."

"I will, dear. Molly is very good about that. Right now, Toby needs a nap every day because of the accident and his recovery. She's sending me to bed for a nap, too."

"Good. I like that."

"She's such a nice young woman. I know the doctor told us she didn't have any family in Florida, but does she have any family anywhere?"

"I don't know. I haven't asked her."

"I'll ask her. She shouldn't be completely alone in the world."

"A lot of people are, Mom. They survive."

"I know, but Molly deserves better."

Richard couldn't argue with that.

"Do you like our tree, Molly?" Toby asked her the next morning at breakfast.

"Very much, Toby. It's huge."

"Did you have big ones when you were little?" he asked.

"Not that big."

Elizabeth looked up. "Do you have brothers and sisters, Molly?"

"No, I was an only child, like Toby."

"Are your parents alive?"

"No," Molly said and smiled at Elizabeth. She appreciated that lady's interest, but she didn't want to tell her life story. There was no need for that.

"Molly's parents died when she was seven," Toby informed his grandmother.

"Oh, no! I'm so sorry!"

"It was a long time ago, Elizabeth. I'm fine."

"Did you go to live with family?"

"No, she lived in a—a what, Molly?"

"A foster home, Toby," Molly said with a sigh. Now she regretted telling Toby about her past.

"But I've heard being in a foster home is awful. Was it bad, Molly?"

"Not bad, Elizabeth. It—it was just not as nice as being with family."

"Well, this Christmas, we're going to be your family!" Elizabeth said with a big smile.

Molly silently groaned. She knew Richard would think she'd put his mother up to that idea. "Really, Elizabeth, that's not necessary. And please don't buy me gifts. I wouldn't be able to reciprocate in kind. I have a small budget."

"Money doesn't matter, Molly. But we've thought of all kinds of ways to celebrate Christmas. I'm supposed to check the times and dates of things Richard thought of last night. He was wonderful."

"How nice. What did he suggest?"

Elizabeth filled her in on all the plans. "And last but not least, we're taking you both to see Scrooge. Would you like that, Toby?"

"I don't know what that is, Grandma," Toby said.

"Oh, of course not, dear. But you'll like it. It's the story of a man who gets a second chance to be good at Christmas, like me."

"You're very good, Grandma," Toby said earnestly.

"Thank you, my angel," Elizabeth said with a big smile. "Oh, do you have a suit?"

"No. My daddy had suits, but Mommy said I shouldn't have one because I would outgrow it so soon."

"Well, I think we should get you a suit for Christmas. We can buy you another one when you outgrow it. Would you like that?"

"I guess so," Toby said doubtfully.

"That won't be your only present, Toby, I promise."

"You mean I might still get a puppy?" The boy couldn't hide his excitement.

"No, Toby, I don't think that's what your grandmother meant," Molly said hurriedly, trying to erase that image from his mind at once.

"Oh."

"Toby, your grandmother is being very nice to you," Molly said softly.

The boy responded by straightening his shoulders and smiling at his grandmother.

"Oh, Toby, you are such a dear boy," Elizabeth said.

"You're a good grandma, too."

Molly encouraged him to finish his breakfast. After he had done so, she sent him upstairs to wash his face and hands.

As soon as he left the room, Elizabeth said, "I know just what to get Toby for Christmas. A puppy!"

CHAPTER FIVE

"ELIZABETH, don't— I mean, don't you think you should discuss such a gift with your son before you say anything to Toby?"

"Why?"

"I appreciate your wanting to make Christmas special for Toby but Richard lives here, too. I don't think you should please Toby at the expense of your son. He loves you and tries to protect you."

"I guess you're right."

Molly was relieved Elizabeth seemed to change her mind. "I'm glad you realize how important your son is in your life."

"Yes, of course. I'll discuss the dog with Richard tonight."

"Elizabeth, have you thought how much a dog could disrupt your household?"

"Louisa?" Elizabeth called. The young woman immediately appeared from the kitchen.

"Yes, ma'am? Do you need something more?"

"Oh, not for breakfast. It was delightful as usual. No, I need to speak to Albert."

Louisa returned to the kitchen. Immediately, Albert appeared in the breakfast room. "Yes, ma'am?"

"Albert, do you know how to train a dog?"

"You mean to go outside and not in the house?"

Elizabeth nodded. "Yes."

"Sure, I can do that."

"So, if we got Toby a dog for Christmas, you could help us with that problem?"

"Yes, ma'am. Is he going to get a dog?"

"Maybe. Do you like dogs?"

"Yeah," Albert said, getting so excited he forgot his usual response. "I always had dogs until—I mean, when I started working for you and your husband."

"You and Delores have your own quarters here, Albert. Couldn't you have had a dog here?"

"No, ma'am. Your husband told me I couldn't."

"Oh, Albert, I'm sorry."

"It's all right, ma'am. He was probably right."

"Well, I'm sure Toby would share his dog with you."

Molly wasn't so sure about that.

"It's not definite, Albert. Elizabeth is going to discuss it with her son," Molly said. "Please don't mention it to Toby."

"No, ma'am, I wouldn't do that."

"Of course not, Albert," Elizabeth agreed. "That's all I needed. I wanted to be able to tell Richard you could help us."

"Yes, ma'am." He hurried back to the kitchen.

"I think this will work out well," Elizabeth said, smiling.

Molly wanted to warn her again, but she didn't think she should. Hopefully Richard wouldn't think this was her idea. If he thought that, he would probably ship her off to Florida before Christmas even got here.

* * *

Richard said goodbye to his happy employees. He'd passed out their bonuses at the party they had just before noon. It had been a good year and he believed in sharing the profits.

Wearily he returned to his office and loaded his briefcase so he could work on his cases at home. Clients being sued didn't care that it was Christmas.

When he got home, his mother and Toby were taking their afternoon naps. Albert had taken Molly to North Park, the shopping mall near their house.

"Do you have anything I could eat for lunch, Delores? All we served at the party were hors d'oeuvres and cakes and cookies. And most of it was gone before I had a chance to nibble."

"Of course, Richard. You want to eat in the breakfast room?"

"Yes, please. I'll go wash up and meet you there."

He often ate a late meal in the breakfast room. It seemed silly to have them serve him in the dining room.

Five minutes later, Delores presented him with a roast beef sandwich with chips and a Diet Coke. Perfect.

As he ate, the silence of the house seemed deafening. Perhaps it was the sharp contrast to the raucous party he'd just left, loud with holiday music and laughter. His employees knew how to kick off their shoes and have a good time, dancing to "All I Want for Christmas" and "Santa Baby" on his secretary's boom box. She'd even asked him to take a turn on the reception area-turned dance floor, but he'd declined. Somehow when he thought of dancing it wasn't his secretary but Molly he saw as his partner.

He'd had to literally shake his head to erase that image. Then and now.

He ripped off a bite of his sandwich, determined to get control of his errant thoughts, when he heard musical laughter coming from the back door. Molly. She'd come into the kitchen with Albert, giggling at some private joke.

Once again the image of her in his arms was being painted by a master right before his mind's eye. She was dressed in red, a slinky, off-the-shoulder gown with high heels; her glowing hair kissed her shoulders, swaying with the rhythm of the music. As they danced, all the other holiday revelers faded away, till there was only them.

Richard lived the fantasy until the real thing appeared at the door of the breakfast room.

Molly came to an abrupt halt when she saw him sitting there.

He cleared his throat. "Good afternoon, Molly." Seeing her laden with packages, he asked, "Did you have a nice shopping trip? Why didn't Albert let you out at the door so you wouldn't catch cold?"

Still standing in the doorway, like a deer caught in the headlights, Molly replied, "I told him it wasn't necessary. After all, I'm not family. I work for you just as he does."

True, he thought, but Albert didn't appear in his day-dreams.

He kept that remark to himself. Instead he voiced, "He should at least carry your packages for you."

"I'm fine." Stepping back, she added, "Now, if you'll excuse me…"

"No." He couldn't let her go. For some reason he wanted her company right now.

What was wrong with him? It wasn't the spiked egg nog

he'd had at the office; there wasn't enough brandy in that to make him act so out of character. Whatever it was, he had to get himself under control. For Toby's sake.

Molly, he noticed, looked at him oddly. Covering for himself, he explained, "I prefer not to eat alone. Why don't you join me? Have a drink, at least." Not waiting for her assent, he called for Louisa and Albert, who appeared almost instantly. He directed Albert to take Molly's packages to her room, and Louisa to bring her a Diet Coke.

Molly tried to think of a way out of being in Richard's company, but she couldn't come up with anything. Toby was napping, as was Elizabeth. And he was her host... and her boss.

Dutifully she sat down—at the opposite end of the table. Apparently that wasn't good enough.

"Why so far away? Come sit next to me." Richard pointed to his left, and Molly reluctantly obliged.

"Your enthusiasm is overwhelming, Molly."

"I'm sorry, but I was capable of carrying my purchases upstairs."

"I'm sure you are, but why not relax and enjoy a drink?"

Louisa entered again and set down a plate of warm cookies.

"See? There's more to enjoy. Thank you, Louisa."

"Albert should be the one receiving the reward," Molly said stubbornly.

"He'll get warm cookies as soon as he gets to the kitchen again." He looked up as Albert entered the room. "You'd better hurry, Albert. Delores just baked cookies."

"I'm on my way." Albert grinned.

"Satisfied?" Richard asked after Albert left.

"Yes, thank you," Molly said, wishing she weren't. She knew Albert didn't have a tough job and that he was well paid. But that didn't mean he should wait on her.

"What did you buy?"

She stiffened. Richard wanted idle conversation? This was so unlike him. "Just some odds and ends," she replied.

"Did you enjoy North Park? I thought Toby might like to see it. Their holiday decorations are usually spectacular. Did they lift your spirits?"

"My spirits didn't need lifting, Richard."

"Oh, right, I forgot. You're filled with the Christmas spirit."

She shoved her chair from the table. "If you'll—"

He grabbed her hand and stopped her departure. "You haven't even touched your snack. You don't want to hurt Delores's feelings, do you?" Then, as if burned, he pulled his hand back. But her forearm still tingled from his touch.

What was going on here? her head screamed. Surely no nurse had that kind of reaction to her boss's touch. She almost chuckled when she thought of Dr. Bradford making her pulse race.

But the sixtyish Dr. Bradford didn't look like Richard Anderson.

Clearing her head, she sat back down. Then, in an effort to save herself, she picked up a cookie, ate it in two bites and drank half her drink. Anything to avoid Richard.

"One cookie won't satisfy Delores."

She looked up at him. Was he kidding?

At her skeptical look, he leaned in close and stage-whispered, "Should I call her in here and ask her?"

Molly leaned back, extending her arm fully to reach another cookie. "Will two satisfy her?" She took a quick bite.

"Maybe, if you take your time to eat it. But if you jump up and run away, not only will Delores be concerned, but my mother will be also as soon as Delores tells her."

Molly closed her eyes. When she opened them she said, "I can't believe you'd really let Delores tattle on me."

"I don't know why. Delores has been tattling on me for at least twenty years." Richard kept smiling.

"Twenty years? Delores has worked here that long?"

"Sure. She had Louisa's job for the first ten years. Then she took over the kitchen when our other cook left. She's been in cahoots with my mom all that time. She thinks she helped raise me."

Against her better judgment Molly smiled. "It probably did take two mothers to raise *you*."

"How many mothers did you have?" he asked.

"Just one," she said succinctly. Her history had already been discussed that day more than she liked.

"Where does your mother live?"

Molly stiffened. Then she said, "Seattle."

"And you didn't plan on going home for Christmas?"

"No, I didn't have the money for a plane ticket. Besides, it wouldn't be worth the trip for just one day." Molly hoped he wouldn't mention her lies to either Toby or Elizabeth. But she refused to pour out her history to this man. The truth made her sound pitiful, and she didn't want Richard's pity. She'd experienced that response many times in the past. Then she'd had to work hard to be treated normally.

"Oh, really? That doesn't sound like a woman filled with the Christmas spirit."

"I'm sorry to disappoint you."

"Feel free to call your mother, if you want. I won't charge you for the call."

"Thank you. That's very generous of you."

He studied her. "But you don't intend to take me up on the offer?"

"I'll call her on Christmas Day on my cell phone."

"I didn't realize you had a cell phone."

"I didn't know I had to tell you if I did," she said, her shoulders stiffening.

"No, it's not necessary. I'm glad to know you keep in touch with your family." Then he lifted the plate of cookies and offered her another one.

"Thank you," she said, taking her third cookie and eating it slowly, as if she were really enjoying it.

"You're welcome." Finally he sat back, giving Molly room to breathe. "What have you planned for Toby for Christmas?"

"I was hoping Delores would let us make Christmas cookies. We could decorate them and even hang some on the tree if Toby wants."

"He might prefer to eat all of them."

"I try to limit his sugar intake. Children tend to get hyper if they have too much sugar."

Richard grinned. "Then I approve of that idea. What else?"

"I had already thought of taking him to the mall."

"Good. Anything else?"

She wasn't going to mention her other idea. He wouldn't understand it. "No, that's all."

"Okay. Well, I'm sure Mom will appreciate your help. She's determined to make this a special Christmas for Toby."

"More than you'll ever know," Molly muttered, thinking about Elizabeth's idea of a dog.

"What did you say?" Richard asked, leaning forward, this time so close she could smell the subtle after-shave that clung to his neck.

"Nothing," Molly said quickly. She had to get out of here. "I've had three cookies, Richard, so I'll go upstairs now, if there's nothing else."

"Fine. I won't hold you. Feel free to leave."

She took him at his word.

After she left, Richard sat there for another few minutes, enjoying another cookie and thinking about her. He had to admit that was about the most enjoyable lunch he'd had in a long time. Then he picked up the two glasses and the plate of remaining cookies and carried them to the kitchen to kiss Delores's cheek and thank her for the quick lunch.

"Did the pretty nurse enjoy the cookies, too?" the dark-haired woman asked.

"She did, but she worries about her weight."

"For no reason."

Right, Richard thought. Her body was perfect, rounded where it should be, with a slim waist and high breasts.

Delores continued, "And she's very pretty."

"Yes, she is." In the right light her red highlights glowed, lighting up her creamy, flawless skin. And those green eyes…

"And kind to," Delores added.

She certainly was, not only to Toby but to his mother. With an easy— He pulled up short. Wait a minute. He knew what was going on here…

"Delores," he said in a warning tone. "Don't be putting

any ideas in my mother's head. I don't want her pressuring me to marry the nurse."

"You are prejudiced against nurses?"

"Of course not. But I've got about all on my plate that I can handle right now."

"Richard, you work too hard. You need to relax and enjoy life more."

He kissed her cheek again. "Right. As long as I make enough to pay your salary, I guess."

"Oh, you!" Delores exclaimed, slapping his arm and laughing.

Richard laughed too and then escaped the kitchen.

He knew his social life the past year and a half had left a lot to be desired. Now that things had settled down at the firm, he'd start rectifying that, right after the holidays. He'd find himself a nice woman, pretty and kind. A woman like Molly.

But the last thing he needed was his mother and Delores playing matchmaker.

Richard was in his home office working before dinner when the door opened and his mother came in.

"Do you have time for a little chat, Richard?"

"Of course, Mom. Are you having any problems?"

"No, of course not. Everything is lovely."

"Good, glad to hear it."

"But the subject of the dog did come up."

"How?"

"I told Toby that I thought we should get him a suit for Christmas. Needless to say, like most little boys, Toby was polite but not enthusiastic. I told him he would get other presents, too. He immediately guessed it was a puppy."

"Did Molly encourage him?"

"Not at all. In fact she deterred him. Even when I told her I wanted to get Toby a dog, she suggested I talk it over with you first."

"She wants to make me the bad guy, I guess."

"No. She just said you should have some say in the matter since you live here, too."

"I could move out if you want me to, Mom. I only moved back home so you wouldn't be alone after Dad died."

Elizabeth shook her head. "I love having you here, and with Toby living with us, I need you to be here. He needs a male presence in his life."

"Okay. So did you agree to talk to me about a dog?"

"Not at first. After all, it is my house."

"It is."

"But she said you loved me and tried to take care of me. She didn't think I should lose you just to please Toby."

"How kind of her."

"She was right, Richard. I was getting carried away," his mother said. "But I still want Toby to have his dog. So I wanted to talk it over with you."

"Okay. What do you want to say?"

"Albert loves dogs and he says he could help us train the dog so it wouldn't make a mess in the house."

"Good for Albert."

"He said your father wouldn't let him have a dog."

"I can believe that. He was a very controlling man as we both know."

"So if he can help us, why can't Toby have a dog?"

"I never said he couldn't, Mom."

"Oh, Richard, you are such a good son!"

"You might change your mind if the dog relieves himself on one of your pricey oriental rugs."

Elizabeth laughed. "A rug is replaceable. And it will make Toby so happy."

"What kind of dog do you want to get him?"

"I don't know. Do you have an idea?"

"One of the attorneys at the office has a dog that just had a litter of puppies about three weeks ago. I think they're chocolate Labs. They're good with children."

"Perfect. Can you call him and get him to sell us one?"

"Sell? I'm his boss!"

"I know, but—"

Richard laughed. "I'm just teasing you, Mom. I'll give him a call right away. Do you want him to keep the puppy until Christmas Eve?"

"Absolutely. I want it to be a surprise for Toby. Can you go get it after he goes to bed?"

"Of course, Mom. Did you ever consider getting me a puppy?" Richard thought of how much he'd wanted one when he was little.

"Yes. I pleaded with your father, but…he didn't like animals in the house. He didn't even want one in the yard. I'm sorry, son." She looked genuinely contrite.

"It's okay, Mom. I grew up just fine without a dog." He reached out for her hand. "I'm just glad we can give Toby one."

"I can't wait to tell Molly that you agree."

"I'm sure it will surprise her."

"Son, you're too hard on her."

"Not all that hard. By the way, I know the doctor told us she had no family in Florida, but did you know she has a mother in Seattle?"

"Oh, no, dear, you're wrong about that. Her parents died in a car crash when she was seven. She told Toby that. And she was raised in a foster home."

Richard frowned. "Maybe she told him that so he'd feel better."

"No, he told me this morning and I sympathized with her. She didn't say anything."

"She couldn't in front of Toby. That would've ruined her bonding with him."

"I'm sure you're wrong. Molly wouldn't lie about something like that."

Richard just shook his head. His mother had never believed bad things about him, either. Unfortunately sometimes he'd lied to her. And he'd always felt so guilt-ridden that he had to admit it afterwards. Maybe Molly would do the same.

"Molly, can I go outside for a little while?" Toby asked after he woke up.

"No, it's too cold outside. You don't want to be sick for Christmas, do you?"

"I guess not."

"Besides, I need you to do something." When Toby looked at her, a question in his eyes, she explained, "Think of something you can give to Richard and your grandmother for Christmas."

"But I don't have any money," Toby reminded her.

"I have some allocated for presents."

"What's allocated?"

"It means I have some money for you for presents."

He seemed to perk up then. "Really? That would be fun."

"Yes, we can go buy them and wrap them up. Then you can put them under the Christmas tree."

"I'd like that. But what can I buy them?"

"Nothing expensive, but maybe some monogrammed handkerchiefs for Richard and scented soap for your grandmother."

"Those aren't very exciting." After a few seconds of silence, during which he gave the subject some thought, his eyes suddenly lit up with excitement. "I bought Daddy a big flashlight. Mommy said he needed it and—" Reality hit him and suddenly those same eyes filled with tears. "I—I forgot he and Mommy aren't ever coming back. Are they?"

"No, honey, they're not," Molly said, reaching out and holding him in her arms. Comfort like this was all she could give Toby, though she ached to take away his pain. Still, she knew it helped to talk about the deceased; that was what everyone had told her. And they were right. Talking about them somehow kept them alive, at least in one's memory. "What did you get your mommy?" she asked him.

"Some perfume," Toby whispered. "I couldn't really afford it," he said, pausing to swallow the tears, "but Daddy said he'd help me 'cause Mommy really, really wanted it."

"I'm sure she would've loved it, baby."

"I—I know." He lay quietly in her arms, the excitement of Christmas lost in his memories of his life in Florida. "Molly, did they die because I wasn't a good enough boy?" he asked anxiously.

Molly hugged him more tightly against her. "Absolutely not. You're a very good boy. It was because someone in another car didn't drive safely. And God gave you your uncle and grandma to make up for losing your parents."

Toby sniffled but said nothing. Molly, her head resting on his soft hair, said, "Did you hear me, Toby? It's important that you know that. It wasn't your fault."

"Okay," he said with a sigh, turning his face into her sweater.

"You're not putting tears on my sweater, are you, Toby?" she asked, trying to put a teasing note in her voice.

"I'm sorry," he said, swiftly moving away from her.

"Oh, sweetheart, I was just teasing. I have other sweaters. I was hoping to make you laugh a little." She stroked his head and wiped away some tears with her fingers.

"I've been trying to be happy for Grandma. She likes it when I smile for her."

"I know she does, and that's very brave of you. But when it's just the two of us, you can cry if you want to. I'll understand."

"Thank you," he said softly and resumed his place against her. "I like the new ornaments we bought, but I wish I had the ornaments from our tree. Mommy helped me pick them out. There was one that had all three of us in a picture frame. And one of me when I was a baby. It was my first Christmas, but I can't remember it."

"I bet you were cute!" Molly said with a chuckle.

"Did you have an ornament like that?"

Molly squeezed him a little tighter. "Yes, I think I did, but—but it gets hard to remember."

"I don't ever want to forget Mommy and Daddy!"

"I don't think you ever will, sweetie. You're a little older than I was and you have that great picture of the three of you."

"Yeah. Daddy threatened to tickle me if I didn't smile at the camera. I wanted to go see Santa instead of having a picture taken. But now I'm glad I did."

"Me, too," Molly said and kissed him on top of his head. "Well, now I need to finish wrapping things so I can put everything away. And if you didn't like my ideas for presents, you can think of something else to get Uncle Richard and your grandma."

"Yeah, I need to think." He left her arms and wandered back into his room.

A few minutes later he ran back in. "We can get Richard a football!"

"Hmm, a football. He told you he likes to play football?"

"No, but I'm sure he would."

"And with whom would he play football?"

"I'll play with him!" Toby said in an excited voice.

"I see. You see, Toby, the art of gift giving is to get the person something he or she wants. Not something you want."

"Oh."

"Want to try again?"

"Yeah," he said, sounding discouraged.

Molly began wrapping the presents she bought that day for Elizabeth, Richard and Toby. They were inexpensive gifts, in hopes that they would enjoy them without feeling the necessity to reciprocate.

Toby wandered back in. "What are you doing?"

"I'm wrapping presents."

"Are any of them for me?"

"Maybe one or two," she told him with a big smile.

"Can I shake them?"

She handed him a box she'd already wrapped. He shook it diligently.

"It doesn't make any noise!" he complained.

"I never said it did," Molly said, grinning.

"Do I have any others?"

"Yes, but they aren't wrapped yet."

"Can I take them downstairs to put under the tree when you get finished?"

"No, sweetie. I'll take them down the night before Christmas. If I take them down early, Richard and Elizabeth might think I'm hoping they'll get me something. That's not why I bought the presents."

"Oh. Will they think that if I buy them something?"

"You're *supposed* to buy them presents. They're your family now."

Toby nodded as he digested the information. Then he looked her straight in the eye as he said, "You know what, Molly? I wish you were my family, too."

Molly had to look away, afraid he'd see the tears glisten in her eyes. When she looked up, Toby was gone.

She never got the chance to tell him she wished so, too.

CHAPTER SIX

RICHARD made arrangements with his friend to pick up a Lab puppy for Toby on Christmas Eve. He hadn't asked his mother if they wanted a male or a female, so he'd chosen a male.

When Louisa knocked on his door to tell him dinner was served, he followed her into the dining room to discover the other three already at the table.

"You must all be hungry," he said with a smile as he joined them.

"Yes, we are," Elizabeth said. "Toby and I napped through our snack today. How about you, Molly?"

Richard raised his eyebrows and stared at Molly, eager to hear her response. She didn't look up.

"I—I had a snack, Elizabeth. Richard was eating when I, uh, came downstairs, and he insisted I join him."

"Well, that was nice of you, son."

"Yes," Richard said, "but Molly wasn't—"

"Very hungry!" Molly said a little louder than usual, cutting Richard off before he could say anything else. This time she glared at him.

So what did Molly not want his mother to know? That

she'd left the house, or that she'd used Albert? His mother wouldn't have complained about either of those things. He'd keep her secret…unless he needed something she didn't want to give him.

He immediately reminded himself he didn't mean it the way it sounded. But she seemed to be good at keeping secrets. Like her mother in Seattle.

Toby's question intruded on his thoughts. "Are we going to decorate the tree this evening, Uncle Richard?"

"Yes, of course. Are you excited about that?"

"I can't wait!"

"Good. Then all we'll need will be some presents to go under it."

"Yes, Molly—"

"Needs to take Toby shopping so he can buy some presents for the both of you," Molly inserted.

Richard could swear her hand was on Toby's leg, warning him not to speak. He checked with the boy. "Is that what you wanted to say, Toby?"

"Uh, yeah. Uncle Richard, do you like football?"

"As well as the next guy. I watch it on Sunday afternoons sometimes."

"No, I mean do you like to throw a football?"

"I haven't done that in a long time, Toby."

"But he played when he was in high school," Elizabeth added.

"Really? Could you teach me how to throw a football?" Toby asked with excitement. "My dad didn't know how."

"I could if we had a football."

Molly jumped.

Richard asked, "Are you all right, Molly?"

"Yes. Toby accidentally bumped into me," she said. "It's no big deal."

Richard looked at Toby's red cheeks. Were they sharing secrets between them? Was that why she'd interrupted Toby earlier? But why would they be arguing about football? That didn't make any sense.

"Would you like for Santa to bring you a football, dear?" his mother asked Toby.

"That would be great, Grandma," Toby replied. "You'll still teach me to throw it, won't you, Uncle Richard?"

"Sure, buddy, I'll do that. Unless it's still this cold outside. If it is, we'll have to wait for a thaw."

"Okay."

"Is there anything else you think you would like for a present?" his mother asked the boy.

Toby immediately looked at Molly and she shook her head.

"Uh, I'd like, uh, some books."

"That's all you can think of?" Richard asked.

"Um, yes. Don't you like books?"

"Sure, I like to read when I have some spare time. That hasn't happened for a year or two, but I keep hoping." He felt Molly staring at him.

"What's wrong, Molly? Does that make me a bad person?"

"No, not at all. I just feel sorry for people who don't read for pleasure."

"Me, too," he agreed with a wry laugh.

Molly looked away.

"Maybe Santa will bring you a book, Richard," Toby said with enthusiasm. Again Molly jerked.

"Is anything wrong, Molly?"

"No, no, nothing's wrong."

"I don't think Santa brings adults presents, Toby."

Toby stared at his uncle. "Really? I don't think so. Mommy and Daddy always got something from Santa."

Elizabeth responded when neither of the other adults had anything to say. "I'm sure you're right, Toby, if the mommy and daddy are true believers."

"Mommy and Daddy were. And I know Molly believes in Santa. And you do, Grandma, because you asked what Santa should bring me. So that only leaves you, Uncle Richard. If you believe in Santa, he's sure to come see us."

"I see. Then I'm sure I believe in Santa, Toby, because I'm sure he's going to come see you."

"And you, too, Uncle Richard. I want him to come see all of us, so we'll all be happy."

Richard exchanged a look with Molly. He could read the gratitude in her eyes. "That's very sweet of you, Toby. I'm sure we'll all receive presents."

"Good. Grandma, what will he bring you?"

"Oh, probably perfume."

"What kind do you wear, Grandma?"

"Chanel No 5. It's terribly expensive, so don't even think of getting me any," she said to Toby.

"Okay," he said with a sigh.

"Is something wrong, dear?"

"No, Grandma. Dinner is really good tonight."

"I'll tell Delores you said that, Toby. She'll be pleased."

"Grandma and I were talking about some fun things to do for Christmas," Richard began.

"You mean the horse and buggy ride? We can do that, can't we?"

"Yes," Richard replied. "And I thought we should go to the North Park Mall and see the decorations while we shop."

Molly shot him a look but he ignored it. "We can all go."

"But how do I buy presents for you guys if you're all with me?"

"I'll take you shopping for their presents, Toby," Molly told the boy, but her eyes never left Richard.

Refusing to back down, Richard said, "We can take turns going with you in the mall, while the others shop. I'd be glad for some all male time."

Toby's face lit up. "You mean just you and me?"

Richard smiled, continuing to watch Molly out of the corner of his eye. She seemed a little perturbed about that.

"Okay. We don't want to go tomorrow because the mall will be jammed on a Saturday. We can go Monday or Tuesday, if you want."

"That would be great!"

"You know, I think maybe the three of you should go. I might get too tired at the mall," Elizabeth said suddenly.

Richard frowned. "You're sure, Mom?"

"Yes, Richard, I'm sure." She smiled at Molly. "I'm sure the two of you can manage with one little boy."

"Of course we can, Mom, if you insist."

Richard looked at Molly. "So is Monday or Tuesday okay with you?"

"Yes, of course, but I can manage with Toby if you have other things to do."

She even smiled at him, which made Richard suspicious. Suddenly she wanted him to avoid doing anything for Christmas with Toby? Or was it him she was trying to avoid? Either way, she was going. "No, I'm looking forward to shopping with you and Toby."

"Certainly," she said, not meeting his glance.

Yep, something was definitely going on.

"Won't it be fun to go to the mall with Uncle Richard?" Toby asked as he was climbing into bed.

"I guess. But I'll give you some money beforehand. Don't spend more than I give you."

"I couldn't, could I?"

"Your uncle might offer you some money, but just tell him you have your own."

"Okay."

"Good. Now hop into bed so I can kiss you good night."

"Okay." After he got into bed, he held up his arms. Molly bent down and hugged him.

As he closed his eyes, Molly turned off the overhead light, leaving just the night-light burning, and hurried into her room. She wanted to finish wrapping the gifts she'd bought today.

She was almost finished when someone knocked on her door.

Immediately she began stowing the bags and packages under her bed. The knock came again. "Just a minute. I have to find my robe," she called. As soon as she had everything out of sight, she hurried to the door.

Richard was standing there. "Nice robe," he commented, raking his gaze over her.

Molly realized she'd forgotten to don her robe over her clothes. "Um, I forgot I was dressed."

Richard looked over her shoulder, but he couldn't see anything suspicious. "What were you doing?"

"I was reading."

"I don't see a book out."

"I—I just finished it."

He braced a hand against the doorjamb and leaned in. "You just seem awfully nervous about something."

"Did you come to my room for a purpose, Richard? Or did you just want to harass me?"

He immediately held up his hands, as if surrendering. "I just wanted to let you know that I told Mom your mother lived in Seattle. She was disappointed that you'd lied to her and Toby."

Molly closed her eyes. Then she opened them. "Fine. Thanks for letting me know."

"What was going on at dinner?"

"I don't know what you're talking about."

"Yes, you do. Toby kept kicking you. And you kept cutting me off."

"I didn't want you to tell your mother and Toby that I had gone to the mall today."

"Why?"

"Toby would be reluctant to take his nap if he thinks I'm going out without him. And your mother might think it was rude of me not to tell her I went out."

"That's a plausible answer, but I don't think it's the real one."

And he was right. But how could she tell him she didn't want anyone knowing about their quiet moments alone? Or, more appropriately, her reaction to those moments?

"Think what you like, Richard. I'm tired and I'd like to go to bed now."

Suddenly his roving eyes caught sight of a piece of red material in the floor. "What's that?" he asked.

She looked over shoulder and then began closing the door. "I need to go to bed now."

She forced him out of the doorway and closed it in front of him. He thought about pounding on the door until she opened it again, but his mother or Toby might hear him. Slipping his hands in his slacks pockets, he strolled down the hall, looking over his shoulder to see if she'd open the door, but it remained shut.

Finally he gave up and went into his room. He had a lot to think about. The nurse was being very secretive, and he couldn't figure out why.

Toby told her first thing the next morning that they'd forgotten to decorate the tree last night.

"You're right, Toby. We'll ask Elizabeth if we can do it this morning."

"Oh, good. Let's go down to breakfast at once."

"Wait a minute. Isn't that the shirt you wore yesterday?"

"Yeah, but I wanted to hurry. It was closest."

"I think you need to change shirts."

"But, Molly, it's hard work changing shirts."

"I'm here to help you."

The little boy turned back into his room. "Okay," he said slowly, indicating how little he liked what he had to do.

It actually didn't take that long, but they were the last ones down for breakfast. Molly hadn't thought about the fact that Richard would be there. He and Elizabeth were sitting at the breakfast table, enjoying pancakes.

"Good morning, dear," Elizabeth said at once. "You, too, Molly. How are you today?"

"I'm fine, Elizabeth. I'm sorry if we're late."

"Nonsense, there's no set time for breakfast, especially not on the weekends."

"Delores?" Richard called. "You've got two hungry customers."

"You want more, Richard?" Delores asked, coming to the door. "Oh, you mean Toby and Molly. I'll have your plates right out."

"Thank you, Delores," Molly called.

"That looks really good," Toby said, staring at his grandmother's plate.

When Elizabeth started to offer him a bite, Molly said, "No, Elizabeth, don't offer him any. He needs to learn to wait for his food. Or maybe he should learn to fix his own breakfast. It would teach him to be patient."

"Oh, don't go that far, Molly. If you do, I'll have to make mine, too. I'd feel spoiled if I didn't at least do as much as Toby." Richard smiled at the little boy.

Toby giggled. "That would be funny, wouldn't it, Uncle Richard?"

"Yes, it definitely would. And Delores would kill us for messing up her kitchen."

"What are you talking about?" Delores demanded as she came through the door. "Who's going to mess up my kitchen?"

"I was wondering if maybe we could make Christmas

cookies one afternoon, Delores," Molly hurriedly said. "But I promise we'd clean up after ourselves."

"Ah, you are a sweet lady, Molly. I guess Toby would like to do that, wouldn't you?"

"It would be fun. I—I used to do that with my mommy," Toby said.

Delores smiled at him. "Of course you can make cookies. I'll help and do the cleaning up myself."

"Thank you, Delores," Molly said softly.

Then Delores set two plates on the table, stacked high with pancakes. "Eat up so you can grow to be a big boy like Richard."

Molly laughed. "But I don't want to be a big boy, Delores. Why did I get so many?"

"So you can keep up with both of them." Delores went back to the kitchen, laughing.

"That'll teach you to challenge Delores," Richard said. "I learned that lesson long ago."

"I'm afraid he's right, dear," Elizabeth said, smiling. "She rules this house."

Having taken her first bite of delicious pancakes, Molly said, "I can see why."

"They're good, aren't they?" Richard asked.

"The best I've ever tasted. Do you know how she makes them, Elizabeth?"

"No, she won't tell me. She doesn't want me in her kitchen cooking breakfast."

After Molly turned to her pancakes, Toby said, "We forgot to decorate the tree last night." He looked at his grandmother, as if knowing he'd get support from her.

"I know, Toby. I realized it last night as I got into bed. But it was too late then. Is this morning all right?"

"Sure. Want to go now?"

"I think you should finish your breakfast first," Richard said, enjoying his second cup of coffee.

"Oh. I don't think I can finish all of them."

"Well, Molly has to finish hers." He shot her a twinkling look. "If she wants to keep up with us."

"Be careful, Richard," Elizabeth called as she stared at her son on the top of a stepladder. Toby and Molly were holding their breaths, too, as Richard put the angel on top of the nine-foot tree.

"I'm fine, Mom. Don't worry. Albert, is that straight?"

"Yes, sir, it sure is. Good job."

"Thanks. I'd rather you be up here instead of me, but Toby insisted."

"Yes, sir, I slipped him a fiver," Albert said with a laugh.

"What's a fiver, Molly?" Toby asked.

"He's teasing, sweetie. He's saying he gave you money to get Richard up on the top of the ladder instead of him."

"But I don't have any money—" Toby said.

Molly hushed him at once. "He's just teasing."

"But—"

Clearly the explanation wasn't working, so Molly tried a diversion. "Have you picked out the first ornament you want to hang, Toby?"

That distracted him, and Molly breathed a sigh of relief. The boy immediately turned to the table with all the decorations. She held her breath, wondering which he would

An Important Message from the Publisher

Dear Reader,

If you'd enjoy reading contemporary African-American love stories filled with drama and passion, then let us send you two free Kimani Romance™ novels. These books will keep it real with true-to-life African-American characters that turn up the heat and sizzle with passion.

By the way, you'll also get two surprise gifts with your two free books! Please enjoy the free books and gifts with our compliments...

Linda Gill

Publisher, Kimani Press

Peel off Seal and Place Inside...

PUBLISHERS
FREE GIFT
SEAL
THANK YOU

THE EDITOR'S "THANK YOU" FREE GIFTS INCLUDE:

▶ Two NEW Kimani Romance™ Novels
▶ Two exciting surprise gifts

YES! I have placed my Editor's "thank you" Free Gifts seal in the space provided at right. Please send me 2 FREE books, and my 2 FREE Mystery Gifts. I understand that I am under no obligation to purchase anything further, as explained on the back of this card.

PLACE
FREE GIFTS
SEAL
HERE

▼ DETACH AND MAIL CARD TODAY! ▶

168 XDL EF2L   368 XDL EF2W

FIRST NAME   LAST NAME

ADDRESS

APT.#   CITY

STATE/PROV.   ZIP/POSTAL CODE

Thank You!

The Reader Service — Here's How It Works:

If offer card is missing write to: The Reader Service, 3010 Walden Ave., P.O. Box 1867, Buffalo, NY 14240-1867

BUSINESS REPLY MAIL

FIRST-CLASS MAIL   PERMIT NO. 717-003   BUFFALO, NY

POSTAGE WILL BE PAID BY ADDRESSEE

THE READER SERVICE
3010 WALDEN AVE
PO BOX 1867
BUFFALO NY 14240-9952

NO POSTAGE
NECESSARY
IF MAILED
IN THE
UNITED STATES

choose. The last Christmas she shared with her parents was the only one she remembered. She'd hung the first ornament, a clear glass ball with the manger scene on it.

Toby had chosen one remarkably like it.

When he picked up that particular ornament, Molly sank her teeth in her lips to keep control of her emotion. Twenty years later and she still got emotional about the holidays.

"You might as well hand me some of the ornaments, Molly, before I get down off this ladder," Richard said.

"All right." She picked up several balls and handed them to Richard.

"One at a time, Molly," Richard said, handing back one of the ornaments.

Which meant she was stuck handing balls to him. Elizabeth and Toby were handling the rest of the tree. Molly said nothing, doing as Richard asked. But she'd hoped to do some decorating herself. She wanted ownership in this tree, too. It had been so long since she'd celebrated a Christmas so gloriously.

"Richard, that's enough balls up there. Come down off the ladder and let Molly hang some of the ornaments, too."

"Sorry, Molly, I didn't think. I would've been glad to trade places with you."

"No, thank you," she hurriedly said, adding in a low voice, "I'm afraid of heights."

"Really?" Richard asked in surprise.

"Yes, really."

"Here, I'll hand you ornaments, how about that?"

"It's not necessary, Richard. Toby's the one who needs to decorate the tree." She didn't want anyone to know how important decorating the tree was to her. Several years, she'd considered buying a big tree just because she'd enjoy decorating it, but she'd talked herself out of it. Money hadn't been plentiful, and in the past couple of years, she'd found other ways of celebrating Christmas. But this year—

"But we want you to have a good Christmas, too. After all, you're not going home for Christmas, either," Richard said casually.

Molly quickly looked at Toby, but he was busy putting an ornament on the other side of the tree. "Please don't say that in front of Toby."

"Oh, sorry, I forgot. That's the problem when you start telling stories."

"The story I told was to you!" she snapped. "I didn't want to tell you my situation. I knew you would make fun of me!"

Richard narrowed his eyes. "You're not serious, are you?"

"Yes, I am!"

"Okay. So hang some ornaments on the tree!"

"Thank you, I will." She blinked rapidly, trying to handle the sudden tears as she helped decorate the beautiful tree.

When they finished decorating, they all stood together, staring at the huge tree.

"It will look even better when we turn the lights on tonight," Elizabeth said. "It will look magical in the dark."

"I think it looks wonderful now," Toby said.

"Me, too," Molly agreed in an awed voice.

For the first time, Richard believed Molly's statement that she'd lied to him, not Toby. He thought the tree was nice, but he'd had big trees as a boy every year. His mother had seen to that. His father hadn't participated in decorating the tree, but his mother and whoever the chauffeur was at the time had helped him and Susan with the tree.

He fought the urge to put his arms around Molly. He'd be crazy if he did such a thing. She'd probably slap his face. His mother would order the wedding invitations.

"Now, Albert, you can put up the other decorations," Elizabeth said in a soft voice, as if she didn't want anyone to notice.

"What decorations, Mother?"

"I got Albert to get some lights to go around the room at the top of the wall. They'll blink like the Christmas tree."

"Oh, that will be lovely, Elizabeth," Molly said.

"Don't you want me to put up these, too?" Albert asked. He held up some greenery.

Richard recognized it at once as mistletoe.

"Mother!" he exclaimed.

CHAPTER SEVEN

IN SPITE of Richard's protest, the mistletoe went up all over the downstairs.

Molly made a mental note not to linger in any doorways. She didn't expect Richard to want to kiss her, but she didn't want to tempt fate. Not that she wasn't attracted to the man. That was part of the problem. She was. But she had no place in their world. Once Toby was settled in, she'd be back in Florida.

She released an unconscious sigh, thinking about the time she had to leave.

"Molly? Is anything wrong?" Richard asked.

They were all having lunch together, again in the breakfast room. Louisa was off for the day to be with her family, and it made things easier for Delores and Albert if they ate there.

"No, what made you think that?"

"You sighed," he said, watching her closely.

"Oh, I was thinking about a friend back home," she hurriedly said.

"A boyfriend?"

Molly shot him a puzzled look. "No."

"No boyfriend waiting for you in Florida? I find that hard to believe."

"A nurse doesn't have a lot of free time, or the energy to do much when she does," Molly said. She took a sip of tea, hoping that would end this ridiculous conversation.

"That sounds like my life. Since my dad died, I've been reworking our law firm, trying to bring it up-to-date and get back on top of the legal world in Dallas. I don't have much free time, and no energy when I do."

"Dear, I knew you were working long hours, but I didn't realize how hard it was for you," Elizabeth said. "I should've paid more attention."

"No, Mom, I'm fine. We're about to get to the point where I can take it a little easier."

"You should take a vacation as soon as you can," Elizabeth said. "I'll be here with Toby, so we'll manage just fine."

"I'm not sure, Mom. You might need me."

"Maybe we could get Molly to come back for a couple of weeks," Elizabeth suggested, looking at Molly expectantly.

"I doubt I'll get any more time off once I get back. My vacation is scheduled for July."

"Oh, dear, that's a long time away. You're not having any fun at all during Christmas," Elizabeth said.

"Yes, I am, Elizabeth. I'm enjoying myself immensely, I promise." Molly gave the woman her best smile. She couldn't let her think she was suffering. In truth, she wasn't. She was getting to do things she'd always wanted to do. Most of all, she was getting to spend time with Toby and know she was helping him adjust to his new family.

"All right, dear. Oh, I know what we should do, Richard. We should all go to lunch at Antares, in the ball."

"Mom is talking about the restaurant located in the ball on the Dallas skyline. You can see the entire area because the restaurant rotates while you're eating."

Molly swallowed. Her fear of heights made that prospect turn her stomach.

"Mom, I'm not sure—" Richard began.

Toby, however, was excited. "That sounds neat. Can we go, Grandma?"

"Yes, dear. I think we could do that Monday and then you three could do your shopping on Tuesday. Yes, that's what we'll do."

Molly said nothing, hoping either she would work up enough nerve to go, or she could plead a temporary illness that would keep her at home.

Richard caught her eye, silently asking if she wanted him to halt the plans. She shook her head. She'd deal with it on Monday.

"I think you need to take Toby to buy a suit today, Richard. Maybe they have something that would fit him, with his casts on. We can have it tailored after he gets his casts off."

Richard agreed. "What are you and Molly going to do?"

"Oh, we'll make some plans, organize our shopping, that kind of thing. We might even go to some stores, if you're not taking Albert."

"No, I'll drive my car. Is that okay with you, Toby?"

"Yeah. I like your car."

"Okay. Then, if you've finished your lunch, let's head out."

Molly and Elizabeth sat there in silence for several

minutes. Then Elizabeth said, "It's a lot quieter when they're both gone, isn't it?"

Molly laughed. "It is, but honestly I miss the noise. Richard is being very good to Toby."

"I think he loves him very much. He loved his sister and missed her when she…left the family. I know they talked once or twice, but he hated his father's behavior. In Florida, you didn't see him at his best. He was mourning Susan's death and trying to take care of me. I'm afraid I'd become quite a burden."

"But you seem to be doing very well now," Molly said, not sure what had brought on the change.

"Yes, I changed my attitude. I had something to live for. Toby needs me. Richard didn't need me, even though he would say differently, but I knew better."

"Then, in spite of the tragedy, I'm glad Toby has come to you and Richard. I know he's going to be happy here with you."

"I hope so. But you've made a big difference, easing him into a role in our home. I know Richard is paying you a lot, but what you've given Toby is priceless."

"Thank you, Elizabeth. Now, you need to rest for a while so I won't have to lie to Richard when he returns."

"I think I will, if you don't mind."

Molly stood as Elizabeth left the room. Then she gathered their dishes and took them to the kitchen so Delores wouldn't have to come get them. She made several trips, before Delores returned to the kitchen.

"What are you doing, child?" the cook demanded.

"I'm helping out. I'm going to load the dishwasher so you have time to do other things."

"Bless you, Molly. With Louisa not here, I'll admit it's a little difficult."

"Well, Elizabeth sent the two men to get Toby a suit and she's gone up to lie down, so I'm free. I'll do anything I can to help you."

"In exchange, I'll give you my recipe for pancakes."

"That's a deal, Delores. I'll be the belle of the ball in Florida if they taste your pancakes."

The rest of the afternoon, Molly worked in the kitchen alongside Delores, helping her prepare dinner for that evening. When Richard and Toby came in, they discovered Molly sharing a cup of coffee with Delores, laughing together at some of the cook's stories about Richard and Susan as children.

"What's going on here?" Richard asked.

Molly smiled at him. "I'm getting some good blackmail material from Delores."

"Delores, you wouldn't betray me, would you?"

"This little girl worked with me all afternoon. I'm giving her my pancake recipe!"

"You wouldn't give it to Mom, but you're giving it to Molly? And what do you mean, she worked in here all afternoon?"

"You know it's hard with Louisa gone. Molly helped me out."

"I thought you were going to make lists with Mom. What happened to that plan?"

"I sent her up to have a nap, and she hasn't come down. Maybe I should go check on her."

As if on cue, Elizabeth asked from the doorway, "What's everyone doing in the kitchen?"

"I was just coming to check on you," Molly said.

"No need. I'm here. But I didn't expect to find all of you in the kitchen."

"You're right, Elizabeth. I can't work with a crowd in here," Delores said.

"My fault. I was hoping I could learn some cooking tricks from Delores. Thanks for letting me visit with you, Delores," Molly said and slipped from the room. "Toby," she called over her shoulder, "come show me and your grandma what you bought."

That quickly cleared the kitchen, except for Richard. He looked at Delores. "She was helping you?"

"Yes. She said she had the afternoon free and knew Louisa was gone. She did the lunch dishes and then helped with the preparation for dinner."

"That was nice of her."

"Nice? That was really sweet of her. You can't find a sweeter person than Molly. Richard, you shouldn't let her get away!"

"Now, Delores, you know I'm kind of busy right now."

"Yes, but that's not important. Molly is what's important."

Richard just smiled and shook his head. Then he excused himself to find the ladies and get their compliments on his job of shopping with Toby. He'd gotten the boy a couple of pairs of slacks, a belt and several dress shirts to go with his suit. And he'd bought him his first tie, and a sweater to wear until his cast was off. It looked better than a jacket that was too big for him.

"Molly, can you tie a man's tie?" Richard asked.

"No, I can't. You'll have to teach Toby that particular skill," she told him.

Richard nodded. "I can do that. When he gets dressed in the morning, I'll tie his tie after breakfast."

"All right. Is he wearing his suit in the morning?"

"We're going to church in the morning. He'll wear his sweater, dress shirt and tie, with one of his new pairs of slacks. Will you join us?"

"Yes, I'd like that."

Richard smiled at her. "Good."

"Would anyone like to go to the movies tonight?" Elizabeth asked. "They're showing a film I'd like to see."

"What is it, Elizabeth?" Molly asked.

She named a current movie. "It's supposed to be quite funny and romantic."

Toby made a face that made Richard laugh. "Sometimes, buddy, we have to go to movies we aren't crazy about to keep the ladies happy. But we can always eat a lot of popcorn."

"I like popcorn!"

"Okay, we'll escort you ladies to the movies tonight. What time does it start?"

Elizabeth told him the time and he went back to the kitchen to make sure Delores could have dinner ready on time.

When he got back in the den, he heard Molly suggest that she and Toby stay home.

"No way. Toby shouldn't have to give up his popcorn, and you need some reward for helping Delores this afternoon."

"She helped Delores? You didn't have to do that, Molly," Elizabeth protested.

"It wasn't much. I enjoyed it."

"We're all going to the movies, Molly," Richard said firmly. "No arguments."

"You'd best go along with him when he uses that tone, dear. It means he's determined." Elizabeth smiled at Molly.

Richard held his breath. He thought she was tempted to challenge him, but he wanted her to go. When she nodded, he silently let out the breath he'd been holding.

When they reached the theater, it was already crowded. To get four seats together, they would have to sit down front. Elizabeth turned to Richard. "Toby and I will take one of the popcorns, and you and Molly take the other one. We're going to take these two seats."

Richard didn't know if his mother was trying to matchmake or didn't really want to sit so close to the screen. Whichever the case, the result was the same. He was going to sit with Molly and share a bucket of popcorn. He couldn't admit to himself the reason his pulse was racing.

They settled into their seats just as the movie started. Richard put the popcorn between them, encouraging Molly to have some. Just then, a big man, weighing at least three hundred pounds, pushed past them to sit in the seat next to Richard.

Richard, uncomfortable, leaned toward Molly.

He whispered, "Sorry but I've got to move closer." Then he raised his arm and put it on the back of her chair.

When Molly saw the man on the other side of Richard, she scooted over as much as she could. Richard lifted the arm of the chair between them and moved even closer.

He told himself it was the only practical thing to do, but as the movie started, he found himself distracted by Molly's warmth and scent. When something funny happened on screen Molly laughed, and her low, sexy chuckle riveted through him.

Damn! He should've taken more time off the past year so he wouldn't leave himself vulnerable to the first woman who walked into his life in two years. This was ridiculous. He wanted to draw back, to remove his arm from around her, but there was no room.

A moment later, she leaned into him. "Don't you want some of the popcorn?"

"Oh, uh, yeah," he said and reached into the tub for a handful of popcorn. Molly got some after him and munched on the popcorn as if totally unaware of him. And he was practically a blithering idiot because he was pressed up against her.

After a while, he relaxed, out of necessity, and began watching the movie. It was funny and not too sappy. When it was over, he stood, along with Molly, and moved out of the auditorium.

The sensation of loss amazed him. He wanted to pull Molly against him and hold her there, but he couldn't do that. They moved out into the lobby and waited for Elizabeth and Toby.

"That was fun," Molly said.

"Yeah, it was." Richard took a deep breath, drawing in Molly's scent. It was a good thing they were getting out of this place.

Elizabeth came out with a sleepy Toby.

Richard moved forward and picked up the little boy. "I think this little guy is just about asleep on his feet."

"Yes, it's quite late for Toby," Molly said. "How did he do, Elizabeth?"

"He enjoyed it until we got about halfway through. I looked over and he was slumped down in his chair. I put his head on my shoulder and let him sleep."

"Next time we'll have to go to an earlier movie," Molly said.

So there'd be a next time? Richard thought. But he said nothing.

As soon as they got home, he carried Toby up to his room, closely followed by Molly and Elizabeth. Elizabeth parted with the others at the top of the stairs.

Molly opened the door to Toby's room and hurried ahead of Richard to turn down the covers. When he lay Toby down, she slipped off his shoes and then his pants. Richard slid down the zipper on his coat and managed to get it off. His shirt was knit and short-sleeved and Richard quickly got it off. Together, they'd managed to undress him in two minutes. The big T-shirt only took seconds.

"We did a pretty good job, didn't we?" Richard whispered with a grin.

Molly smiled back but she was busy covering the little boy up and kissing his forehead.

Richard was jealous. When that thought struck him, he took a step back. What was wrong with him?

"He was exhausted," Molly whispered. "Thank you for carrying him upstairs, Richard."

"No problem. Are—are you going to bed now?"

"Yes, I think I will. Good night," she said softly and stood there waiting for him to leave.

Damn it, where was the mistletoe when he needed it? "Good night. I'll see you in the morning."

He backed out of the room, finally breathing when he

closed the door. He took the long walk down the hall to his bedroom. He obviously needed some time to think. He'd been too close to Molly tonight and it had screwed up his defenses.

He just needed some time alone to resurrect his defenses. He didn't need a woman intruding into his life right now.

Molly had watched Richard's entry into his bedroom. Once he was out of sight, she slid out of Toby's room and tiptoed down the hall to the stairs. She wanted to see the Christmas tree in the darkened room, the lights shining like stars in the sky.

When she entered the garden room, she found the plug and turned on the lights. With a deep sigh, she sat down at the glass table, staring at the tree, perfect in her mind, and the lights glowing around the walls. The entire room seemed magical, as Elizabeth had predicted.

Molly sat there, soaking in that magic, the ephemeral lightness filling her soul. Maybe next year she would get a big tree, though not this big, so she could sit at night and enjoy the gleaming lights. Then she wouldn't have to sneak down to enjoy Christmas.

A slight noise awakened her from her dreams. She whirled around to discover Richard approaching. "What— what are you doing here? You went to bed!"

"You said you were going to bed, too."

"So you're spying on me? Do you want me to pay for the electricity I'm using?" She regretted her words as soon as she spoke. Richard and his mom had been more than generous to her. "I'm sorry. I shouldn't—"

"No, you shouldn't have. I came down to make some

coffee and saw the lights on. I thought maybe Albert had forgotten to turn them off."

"I'll turn them off now," she said, jumping up from her chair.

"I have a better idea," he said. "I'll go make some decaf coffee for both of us and we can enjoy it in here."

"Really, I should go to bed. There's no need—"

Instead of answering her, he bent down and brushed her lips with his. "Watch the lights," he said and walked out of the room.

Molly was completely flustered by that brief kiss. Why had he done that? Had he thought she'd flirted with him at the movies? She'd worked hard to make sure her voice sounded normal, even though he was pressed against her. She knew one thing. For all his complaints about lack of time, he'd found some time to work out somewhere. He was solid muscle.

She flushed from her head to her toes, glad he wasn't in the room. Even in the darkness, he might've noticed her blush.

Within minutes Richard appeared in the doorway, carrying two mugs of coffee. He set one in front of Molly and he took the seat next to her, pulling it even with hers. "We did a good job, didn't we?"

"Yes! The tree is beautiful," she said breathlessly.

"Are you okay?"

"Yes, of course. I just wanted— I enjoy seeing the tree at night. As your mother said, it's magical."

"I realized that when I saw you staring at it today. You were remembering trees in the past, weren't you?"

All she could do was nod.

"When did your parents die?"

She turned to stare at him. "You believe me now?"

"Yeah, I believe you. I'm not sure why you lied to me, but I believe you."

Abruptly she said, "I was seven."

"And you went to a foster home?"

"Several foster homes," she muttered.

Richard frowned. "Why did you change?"

"Well, let's see, in the first foster home, the dad was caught forcing himself on a couple of the older girls. So we were all moved to different homes. It's like starting all over again. The second foster home closed down because the mom won the lottery and didn't need the money she got from the state."

"She didn't mind letting you go?"

Molly gave a cynical laugh. "She dumped us so fast it made our heads spin."

"Then what happened?"

"My third foster home I stayed in until I was eighteen. By then I'd worked for three years and had saved as much as I could."

"What kind of work?"

"I was a telephone operator, part-time."

"How did you get into nursing?"

She shrugged a shoulder. "I got a scholarship. It didn't pay for everything, but most of it. I paid for the rest."

"And how—"

"No more questions about me. It's your turn. Was your dad as awful as he seems?"

"He was difficult. I try not to say too much, because I think Mom loved him, but he was controlling, self-centered. I managed to get along with him, but he considered females to be second-class citizens. Susan wouldn't buy that attitude. She fought him all the way."

"Good for her," Molly whispered.

"When my father tried to tell her who to love, that was the last straw. She moved to Florida with Kevin, Toby's father, and never came back. My father disowned her after that."

"I'm sorry, Richard." Sympathy was audible in her voice. "That must have been hard on you."

"Yeah. I called her a couple of times, but she obviously wouldn't come home for a visit, after Dad cut her out of his life. It was stupid on his part."

"Yes, it was." She sat there for a minute staring at the Christmas tree. Then she said, "Life's too short for such silliness."

"As we both know," he said softly. Then he stretched his arm on the back of her chair.

She thought about moving away, but the warmth of his arm felt good. They sat there in silence, looking at the tree. Molly had enjoyed the lights before he came down, but they were always better when shared.

After a few minutes, he pulled her a little closer and her head rested on his shoulder. They remained there for a long time. Somehow, in the darkness, she didn't feel like it mattered.

Molly enjoyed his closeness, but she knew when daylight came, the magic would end.

Molly enjoyed the visit to their church the next morning. They only went to the main service in the large auditorium, where the minister gave an intelligent and entertaining sermon.

The only thing that bothered Molly was that Elizabeth again took Toby's hand and led him into the pew first. Which left her between Toby and Richard. At least they didn't have to separate, leaving her with Richard. And they had plenty of room in their pew.

They went out to lunch after the church service since Delores had the day off.

"We should've gone to Antares today," Elizabeth said as they ate lunch at a local restaurant. "But I made the reservations for Monday."

"That's okay, Mom. I like the pies here."

"Richard, I don't know how you stay so lean, with all the desserts you eat. It's disgusting!"

Molly thought so, too, but she wasn't going to make any comments.

"I went to the gym every morning this past year, Mom. That's how I can eat all those desserts. And I enjoy every one of them."

"Maybe I should get up and go with you," Elizabeth muttered.

"You look lovely, Elizabeth. You have nothing to worry about," Molly assured her.

"Yes, but I pass up the desserts most of the time."

"It's probably better for you," Molly said, smiling in sympathy.

"So you're both going to pass up dessert?" Richard asked incredulously.

Molly looked at Elizabeth and at the same time they said, "No way!"

Richard grinned. "Looks like we're all having pie, right, Toby?"

"Can I have ice cream instead?"

"Sure, buddy, if that's what you want."

Toby nodded enthusiastically.

Molly again realized how close Richard and Toby were becoming. By the time she left, she thought Richard would be regarding Toby as his own son.

Toby would scarcely miss her.

She chastised herself for that thought. That was what she should hope for. And she should hope that she wouldn't miss Toby…or anyone else when she went back to Florida.

Maybe she should look for a job here in Dallas? No, no, that wouldn't be a good idea. She needed to cut her emotional ties to Toby at once. It would be easier that way.

"Hey, they have a Christmas tree here!" Toby called out.

"Yeah, they do, but it's not as pretty as ours, is it, Toby?" Richard asked.

"Ours is the best! Do they have one at the mall?"

"They always have at least one," Richard said, looking at Molly.

She knew he was thinking she should've answered the question since she'd been to the mall. "Didn't you go to the mall to get Toby's new clothes?"

"No, we went to a men's store at Highland Park Village, where we went to the movies last night."

"We're fortunate that we have a lot of specialty shops around here," Elizabeth said with a smile. "Whatever we're looking for, we can find nearby."

"How nice," Molly said. In her mind, she was thinking, "If you can afford it!"

Then, at Elizabeth's horrified glance and Richard's grin, she realized she'd spoken her thoughts aloud.

CHAPTER EIGHT

"Oh, I'm so sorry. I didn't mean to say that out loud!" Molly said, her voice filled with anguish. "You've both been so good to me, treating me like family, and I have no reason—"

Richard reached over and touched her hand. "It's okay, Molly. Mom didn't think about the fact that you might not be able to afford the shops around here."

"I don't have to be able to afford them. I'm not shopping for anything. I shouldn't have been so rude."

Elizabeth smiled at her. "Don't worry about that, Molly. I'm very fortunate and sometimes I forget that others don't live like I do. It's a good reminder to me."

"But I shouldn't have reminded you of that, Elizabeth."

"Let's call it quits on that subject, dear. Toby is ready for his ice cream and I'm going to choose my pie. What kind do you want?"

"I love apple, especially if it has a scoop of ice cream on it," Molly said, smiling.

"Hey, I didn't volunteer to pay for ice cream for you, young lady," Richard said, laughing at her.

"Richard!" Elizabeth exclaimed.

"Just teasing, Mom. I'll even pay for you to have ice

cream. It's all Toby's fault, of course. He's the one who mentioned ice cream first."

"But I didn't want pie!" Toby protested.

They all burst into laughter, which confused both Toby and their waiter.

"Come along, everyone. We don't want to be late for lunch at Antares," Elizabeth called.

Molly looked at Toby, dressed in some of his new clothes. "You look very nice, honey, but I think I'm going to stay home today."

"No, Molly, I don't want to go without you."

"You'll be fine. Richard will be there."

"No. I won't go if you don't."

Molly swallowed. She'd gotten ready for the lunch trip to downtown Dallas, but at the last minute, she didn't think she could go. "Toby—"

"Molly, Toby, come on. Richard is waiting."

"Come on, Molly," Toby said, pulling her hand as he headed toward the door of his bedroom. "We've got to hurry."

Molly gave up and followed him into the hallway. They reached the head of the stairs when Elizabeth came into view.

"Oh, there you are! Richard is waiting in the car. It's much warmer today than it was, but still, we don't want him to get impatient."

"No, of course not," Molly said, trying to forget their destination.

They hurried outside and got into Richard's SUV.

"I was beginning to think I was going by myself," Richard said as he backed out of the driveway.

Molly, sitting in the front seat, said nothing.

Elizabeth said, "Toby wasn't quite ready."

"I wasn't?" Toby asked.

"Actually, I was the slow one," Molly said in a hurry.

Richard looked at Molly. "No problem. It won't take us long to get there."

"Oh, good," she said faintly.

"You'll just love the restaurant, Molly. It's part of the Hyatt Regency Hotel. Very stylish," Elizabeth commented.

"I'm sure it's lovely, Elizabeth."

"Can we see our house from there, Uncle Richard?"

"With all the trees, probably not. But we can see the American Airlines Center where our pro basketball team plays. And we'll see the Trinity River, and the rest of downtown. We might even be able to see Six Flags Over Texas. I can't remember ever looking for it, but we'll try today."

"What is Six Flags Over Texas?"

"It's an amusement park, Toby," Elizabeth explained.

"Can we go there, too?" he asked.

"It's closed during the winter. You might get to go next summer."

"Molly, will you want to go, too?" Toby asked.

"No, probably not, Toby."

"Why not?"

Molly pasted on a smile as she looked over her shoulder. "Because I'll be back in Florida by then, Toby."

"Uncle Richard, does Molly have to go back?"

"Toby!" Molly exclaimed before Richard could answer. "I have to go back. There will be other children who are hurt and need me."

"But I need you."

"No, you have Richard and your grandmother, Toby. Remember?"

"Yeah, I guess so," he said sadly.

"Your grandma has planned a nice day for you, Toby. Don't ruin it for her," Molly said gently.

"No, I won't. Thank you, Grandma."

"Toby, look, there's where we're going," Richard said, pointing out a large ball up in the air, sitting on concrete pillars.

"Do we have to walk up there, Uncle Richard?"

"No, there's an elevator." He pulled the car into the driveway of the Hyatt Regency Hotel and stopped. "We're doing valet parking, so hop out, everyone."

Molly got out, but she didn't want to. She wanted to offer to drive around the block a couple hundred times until they came back down, but she knew Richard wouldn't allow that.

He led the way down a long escalator and Molly wondered why they were going down when the restaurant was up on top. But then they reached a bank of elevators. When the doors opened, Richard led them in.

Molly faced forward, prepared to close her eyes until they reached their destination. Behind her, Toby was chatting with Elizabeth.

Suddenly he said, "Look, Molly!"

Immediately Molly turned around only to see that what she'd thought would be the back of the elevator was actually a bank of windows that looked down on the quickly disappearing ground.

Just as her knees buckled, Richard's arms went around her and he pressed her face into his chest. "Don't look, Molly. Just stay here with me. We'll be there in a minute."

"I'm sorry to be such a coward," she whispered, on the verge of tears.

"It's not a problem. Toby doesn't understand. Neither does Mom."

"Why do you?"

"I've had an illogical fear or two. My dad insisted I get over them. As much as I tried, I couldn't."

"No, it's not something you can control."

"I was watching you, afraid you'd get upset, so I knew at once when you turned around, you weren't going to make it."

"Can I go back down?"

"Not now. We have to eat first. But don't worry, you won't have to sit by the window. I'll sit there, and I'll keep you safe."

"Thank you." Just as she said that, she heard the elevator door open. She raised her head and looked over her shoulder just as he eased her forward and out the elevator door.

Richard gave their name to the hostess who took them to their table. Richard held Molly back and let his mother and Toby go first.

When they stepped down on the lower level of the restaurant floor, Richard kept his arm around her and he steadied her with his other hand when she realized the floor was moving.

"Easy," he whispered. "We'll be at the table in a minute."

When they reached the table, Richard went in first so he had the window seat opposite Toby, and he pulled out the chair next to him for Molly.

"Richard, you should give Molly the window seat. She'll want to see everything," Elizabeth told him.

"Mom, Molly is afraid of heights. She'll be all right in

the chair she's in. If she wants to see anything closer, all she has to do is tell me."

"Oh, Molly, why didn't you say anything?"

"I—I didn't want to spoil everyone's fun," Molly said.

"Poor dear. Do you want us to leave now?"

"No, it's all right. Richard has promised to make it easier for me when we go down, so we might as well eat before we do that."

"You're being very brave. Isn't she, Toby?"

"Yes, but it's my fault," Toby said, tears forming in his eyes. "I told her I wouldn't come without her."

"Toby, it's okay," Molly said, reaching across the table to touch his hand.

Richard looked at the boy. "You need to be more thoughtful of others, Toby.

"Richard, don't. He's just a little boy!"

"Yes, but I don't think he realized how difficult it would be for you." He stretched his arm around her chair, as he had the night they'd watched the lights together.

"He's just come through a terrible ordeal. He'll be more thoughtful in the future."

"Okay, buddy," Richard said, reaching over and patting Toby's arm. "I know you're just a little boy. But part of growing up is learning to think about others."

"Okay," Toby whispered.

"Good, now we need to order," Elizabeth said. "Toby, what do you think you would like?"

"A cheeseburger," he replied without hesitation.

"You know what, Toby?" Molly asked. "I'm going to have the same." She smiled at the little boy.

The waiter came and they placed their orders. He

brought their drinks at once and Molly took a sip of her Diet Coke. It helped her feel a little better.

"Uncle Richard, did you look for the amusement park?"

"Not yet. Let's see, there's the Trinity River, so we're facing south right now. When we rotate west, we can look for it."

"How will we know?" Toby asked.

"There'll be a sign painted on the wall that says West."

"Okay, I'll watch for it."

Now that Toby's attention was off her, Molly slumped in her chair.

"You okay?" Richard whispered, leaning closer, his breath warm on her skin.

"Yes, but you shouldn't have blamed Toby," Molly returned.

"I won't have him spoiled by you and my mother. He has to learn to be responsible for his actions."

"I agree, but it seems a little harsh so soon after he lost his parents." She should know; she'd experienced that first-hand.

"I didn't beat him, honey. I just pointed out what he had done. I don't think that's too harsh."

"Well, I do, *honey!*"

"But you're not in charge of him. My mother and I are."

Molly's gaze fell to the table. She refused to look at him. She knew she wasn't in charge of Toby, but she cared for the boy. Surely Richard knew that. At the moment, she disliked Richard. And truthfully she didn't want to leave Toby with him.

"Was that truth too harsh, too?" Richard asked, watching her response.

She nodded, trying to hold back tears. She knew she was

too emotionally involved with Toby. Even with Elizabeth and Richard. Especially with Richard if she were honest. It seemed they shared a lot recently. So much for her vow to avoid him. She was used to being alone, and it was going to be difficult to forget her visit to Texas.

He pulled her a little closer to him, but she didn't rest her head on his shoulder like she wanted to. She didn't really have that right.

"Uncle Richard, look, it's here!" Toby exclaimed. "We're facing West!"

Richard responded to Toby, but Molly didn't look up. She could tell Toby was doing just fine. Could it be true, what Richard had said? Still, she wasn't going to admit to him that he was right.

The waiter brought their food. It was all beautifully served and looked great on the plate. Even though a hamburger was the normal American fare, it tasted better than any Molly had ever had. All in all, she had to admit, she enjoyed the lunch at one of Dallas's main tourist attractions.

Until they had to enter the elevator again.

She was still irritated with Richard, in spite of Toby's quick recovery. She was determined to manage without his help. But just entering the elevator, facing the windows for that brief walk, was hard.

When she hesitated, Richard took her hand and turned her around. "You can back in. I'll guide you."

"Thank you," she said stiffly.

Once they were in the elevator, she stood close to the door, her gaze fastened on it, waiting for it to open again.

"Need any help?" Richard whispered.

"No, thank you, I'm doing fine."

"Too bad. I enjoyed our ride to the top."

She said nothing. With her teeth gritted, she refused to bury her face in Richard's chest, as she'd done earlier. She wanted to. His warmth had felt good. But she mustn't take advantage of his goodness.

When the elevator door opened, Molly drew a deep breath of relief, knowing her ordeal was over.

Richard took her hand and led her to the escalator. She tried to pull her hand free, but she would've had to make it obvious to do that. With Elizabeth and Toby right behind them, she thought the best thing to do would be to wait until they reached the hotel lobby. He'd have to present their parking ticket to get the car pulled up.

When that happened, she turned back to Elizabeth and Toby. "Elizabeth, do you want me to sit in the back of the car with Toby on the way home?"

"Do you mind, dear? I'm feeling a little sleepy after our lunch. I believe I ate too much."

Toby took her hand. "Yeah, I'm tired, too."

"I guess you and Grandma both need your rest, don't you?" Molly said. "You were up way too late on Saturday night."

"Yeah, I don't remember the end of the movie."

"That's because you fell asleep. Richard carried you to bed."

"I didn't know that. He must be very strong," Toby said, a touch of awe in his voice.

"I suppose," Molly agreed, but she knew how strong he was. She'd felt his arms around her, too.

Not only did she remember the rock-hard wall of his chest, but she recalled his warmth, the security he provided her in the circle of his arms, the smell of his citrus aftershave. All things she should *not* be remembering now. Shaking off the thoughts, she got in the car and put her head back, willing them not to invade her mind again.

After a few minutes, her roving eyes betrayed her, landing on the rearview mirror where she studied Richard's reflection. His jaw was square, his dark hair perfectly groomed, his blue eyes focused on the road ahead. Say what you will, she thought, but he was one handsome man.

As if feeling her gaze on him, he looked up into the mirror and their eyes met in reflection. "You okay back there?" he asked.

"Y-yes," she stammered, feeling as if she were caught doing something illegal. "I'm fine. Toby's just a little tired."

"We'll be home in a few minutes."

When they got home, Molly roused a sleeping Toby and led him in, holding his hand all the way up to his room. Elizabeth accompanied them upstairs.

A few minutes later, Molly slipped back down. The door to Richard's study was closed. Even so, she tiptoed past the door. When she reached the kitchen, she found Albert sitting at the table having a cup of coffee.

"Albert, could you take me shopping for a few minutes?"

"Sure I can, Molly. You have more Christmas shopping to do?"

"Yes, just a little bit that I can't do at the mall tomorrow."

"No problem. Are you ready to go?"

"Yes. Can we go without asking Richard?"

Albert grinned. "Sure. He doesn't ever need me."

About an hour later, Molly hurried back up the stairs.

She heard a door open as she reached the top of the stairs, but she didn't turn around to see if Richard had come out of his office.

She didn't want to know.

Richard watched Molly's rapid ascent up the stairs, carrying a package. With a frown, he walked to the kitchen.

"Albert, did you take Molly out?"

Albert, sitting at the table with a fresh cup of coffee looked up in surprise. "Yes, sir, I did. Did you need me?"

"No, I was just curious. We're going shopping tomorrow."

"I know, but she had some shopping to do that she couldn't do in the mall."

Richard stood there staring into space.

"Want a cup of coffee, Richard?" Delores offered.

"Yeah, that would be great."

She poured him a cup of coffee, but instead of leaving, Richard sat down beside Albert. "Where did you take her?"

"To a camera store."

"She's buying a camera?"

"I don't know. I didn't go in the store with her. She told me she wouldn't be long, and she was right."

"It seems to me she has a lot of secrets."

Delores chuckled. "Of course she does. It's Christmas. Are you telling everyone what you're doing every moment of the day?"

Delores had a point.

"She's such a nice lady," the cook continued. "I wish she didn't have to leave."

"Toby feels the same way, Delores."

"So why don't you do something about it, Richard?"

"What do you want me to do? Hire a nurse as a nanny to Toby? He's not that small."

"I don't know. I just know I'll miss her when she's gone."

"When is she supposed to leave?" Albert asked.

"Mid-January," Richard muttered and took a sip of coffee. The longer she was here, the more he was dreading the date. But he couldn't admit that to Delores and Albert.

"She sure is pretty," Albert said.

"You got a crush on her?" Richard teased.

"Of course not. I'm old enough to be her father, but I like her. She's kind to everyone."

"Yeah, she is."

"And she's not a snob, like some people you know," Albert added.

"Okay, I get the picture. You both want Molly to stay. But I'm not able to take that on. I'm still working nonstop on office stuff, except for when I have to take Mom, Toby and Molly to do something for Christmas."

"It's about time you slow down. You don't want to be like your daddy," Delores said.

"No, I don't. But I have an obligation to the law firm. A lot of people depend on our success, not to mention the two of you. It would be hard if Mom had to start doing the cooking!"

"Well, you're right, but she could do more. It would probably be good for her. Toby is good for her," Delores pointed out.

"I know. I'm trying to keep him from being spoiled with two women fawning over him."

Delores grinned. "That's a hard job."

"I know. I upset Molly today. She hasn't forgiven me yet, but she will."

"How do you know that?" Delores wanted to know.

"Because Molly can't hold a grudge. It goes against her very nature. You know that."

"Yes, but I don't want you taking advantage of her!"

"So you want Toby spoiled?" Richard demanded.

"No. He's a fine little boy. Susan did a good job."

"Yes, she did. But it would be easy for him to get spoiled in this house."

Delores sighed. "I suppose you're right, but try not to offend Molly. I don't want her to leave."

"I know. Toby and Mom say the same thing. But none of you has come up with a way for Molly to stay."

"I have," Delores said. "You just marry her!"

"Don't be—" He stopped as he heard footsteps behind him. He spun around and saw Molly entering the kitchen. "Molly!" Had she heard Delores's comment? He searched her face and saw no reaction. Feigning innocence, he asked, "What are you up to?"

"I thought I might see if Delores needs any help again today."

The cook smiled. "No, I don't, but I appreciate the thought. Louisa should be here at two o'clock to help prepare dinner."

"She had a long weekend, didn't she?" Molly said with a smile.

"Yes. Her sister got married yesterday."

"How nice."

"Yes, it is. Do you like weddings?"

"Yes. I've only been to a couple, but they always fill me with optimism. You can see the hope on everyone's face."

"Half the marriages today end in divorce," Richard said.

"So people shouldn't get married?" Molly challenged.

"I don't think it's anything someone should rush into."

"I saw a report that couples who date for a long time are less likely to have a lasting marriage than those who marry more quickly." Molly crossed her arms over her chest, as if waiting for him to disagree with her.

"I read that study, too. I'm not sure I believe it, but they had some good points," he said calmly.

"It's time for you to get married, Richard," Delores chimed in. "After all, you're thirty." Then she looked at Molly. "How old are you, Molly?"

"I didn't think you were supposed to ask a woman her age," Richard pointed out.

Molly ignored him. "I'm twenty-seven, Delores."

"Perfect," Delores said with a smile.

Molly raised her eyebrows. "What's so perfect about being twenty-seven?"

Richard had understood Delores's comment, but he challenged her with his stare to explain what she meant to Molly.

Delores was unfazed. "I just think it's a good age. You're old enough to know your mind, but young enough to have some choices."

"I suppose." Molly got up. "I'm going to get some coffee."

"How about a piece of chocolate cake to go with it?"

"You holding back those sweets again?" Albert mock-complained. "What about for me too? And Richard?"

Richard nodded. He was in the mood for sweets, all right. One by the name of Molly Soderling.

CHAPTER NINE

THE afternoon coffee klatch was in full swing in the kitchen, Molly having taken a seat at the table with Richard, Albert and Delores, when Toby walked in.

"Molly? I tried to wake up Grandma, but she didn't want to get up."

Rising immediately to her feet, Molly said, "I'll go see if she's feeling all right."

Richard held his hand out to the boy. "I'm sure she's just tired," he explained. "Why did you want Grandma anyway?"

"'Cause she told me to come to her room when I got up and she'd read to me."

"Oh, that's right," Molly said. "She'd found a book you used to like her to read to you, Richard. She wanted to do the same for Toby." She ruffled the boy's dark hair and smiled down at him. "I'll just go check on her." With that, she left the kitchen.

"Is Grandma sick?" Toby asked Richard, concern in his voice.

"If she is, Molly will fix her up. After all, she's a nurse, isn't she?"

"I hope so," Toby said.

Richard could see the fear in his eyes. He hesitated to reassure him any more. After all, he didn't know if his mother was well. After his father's death, she was severely depressed, but she'd been so much better after they brought Toby home. He hoped she hadn't overdone.

Molly hung up the phone just as Louisa entered the room after a soft knock. "Is she all right?" the maid whispered.

"Oh, Louisa, you're here."

"Yes, I just arrived. How is she?" She nodded to the bed.

"I think she has the flu. I talked to her doctor and he's going to call in some medicine for her to take. Do you know her pharmacy?"

"Yes. Shall I tell Albert to go get it?"

"Yes, please. And do we have some Tylenol? She has a headache and is running a fever."

"Yes, ma'am. I'll get it." Louisa hurried into the bathroom and came back with a glass of water and the medicine.

"Thank you, Louisa."

When Louisa left, Molly put some pillows behind Elizabeth, then she managed to get her to take the Tylenol.

As she lay her back on the pillows, Elizabeth opened her eyes. "Where's Toby?" she whispered.

"He's downstairs. Don't worry about him. Why didn't you say you weren't feeling well?"

"I thought a nap would take care of it. What's wrong with me?"

"Your doctor said it sounds like the flu that's going around. He said to push the fluids and he would prescribe a pill that has helped some of his patients. But basically, you're going to be sick for four or five days."

"But it's Christmas!"

"Actually, it's not Christmas until a week from today. You should be feeling fine by then."

"But I have some shopping I need to do."

"I'll do it for you, or Richard can. Don't worry about things like that."

"I guess so. But I was going to read to Toby from a book Richard used to like."

"I know. I can read it to him in here, so you can see his reaction, if you want."

"Maybe later."

"Okay. Why don't you go back to sleep, and I'll check on you later."

Molly left her alone. As she pulled the door behind her, she almost ran smack into Richard's chest. She would have, if not for his strong arms that held her a foot away.

"How's Mom?" he asked.

"I gave her some Tylenol and she's gone back to sleep." When was he going to let her go? She wondered.

"I want to thank you for calling her doctor."

"No problem." She stepped back and he dropped his arms to his side. "She should be okay in a few days, but I'm going to have Albert pick up some masks. If you go in to see her, I want you to wear one."

"Is that really necessary?"

"It can't hurt."

"Okay."

"She was worried about doing some Christmas shopping. I'll be glad to pick up anything she knows she wants, but you might be better able to help her in that department."

"Okay. I'll talk to her the next time she's awake."

Molly nodded and walked past him.

"Where are you going?" he asked.

"I need to make a list of things I need for Elizabeth."

"If Albert is gone already, I'll go get whatever you need." He followed her back downstairs. "I've got paper and pen in my office," he said, opening the door to his office for her. "Come on in here."

She shrugged her shoulders and followed him in. It was a lovely room, with a lot of bookshelves and leather-bound volumes. A large desk dominated the room, but there was also a leather sofa with a coffee table in front of it. Molly sat down on the sofa and waited.

Richard pulled several pieces of blank paper out of a drawer and took a pen off his desk. He brought them to Molly and sat down beside her.

Though she was a bit unnerved by his closeness, she made her list. She made a note to ask Delores if she had any soup on hand.

"Delores can make some chicken soup," he said as he read her paper. "She'll be happy to."

"Good. Then this should do it." She handed Richard the list. "You know, I can come with you, if Albert has already left. Just let me check on Toby."

In the kitchen she spotted Toby munching a piece of chocolate cake. There was no sign of Albert, who'd apparently already gone.

Richard told Delores he was going to the store. "Want to go with me, Toby?" he asked the boy.

"Can I, Molly?" Toby asked, eagerness in his voice.

Molly looked at Richard. "Are you sure you want to take him along?"

"I thought it would give him something to do."

"Then maybe I should go with you."

"If you're coming, let's go," Richard said, holding Toby's hand in his. "We men are ready to go."

"You *men*?" Molly questioned with a grin.

Richard grabbed her hand with his free one. "Come on, young lady, or you'll be left behind."

In spite of the purpose of their shopping, the threesome had an enjoyable time. Richard wanted to get everything necessary to make his mother comfortable. In addition, because he knew Toby would need ways to pass the time, he found some puzzles and some videos for the boy. When he was about to add a game to his pile, Molly tugged on his sleeve. "Santa," she whispered.

He knew what she meant, and put the game back.

"Besides," Molly said, "I think you've bought enough. We don't want Toby to get spoiled, after all."

Richard looked at her smug expression. He knew she was paying him back for what he'd said earlier in the day.

The store clerk who had been helping them looked at Toby.

"Parents always worry about that kind of thing," he said, grinning at Toby.

"But they're not—"

"Arguing," Richard inserted. "We're not arguing. We're just trying to do the right thing. Right, honey?" He raised one eyebrow in Molly's direction.

"Yes, that's true, *honey*. Are you ready to go, Toby?"

"But we didn't buy that book you said you would read to me."

"*Charlotte's Web*?" Molly asked.

"Yeah, that one."

"Santa might bring it to you, so we'd better wait."

"Oh, okay."

As Toby walked a few steps ahead of them back to the car, Richard grabbed Molly's hand. "Santa has apparently been busy already. I didn't know my mother had done any shopping already."

"You never know." Molly didn't look at him, catching up with Toby to leave him behind.

He stared at her. He was learning to read Molly fairly well. There was something she wasn't telling him about the Santa items, but he wasn't sure what. Probably his mother had made her promise to say nothing.

When they got back to the house, Molly asked Richard to bring the humidifier upstairs to his mother's room. She took the glass of juice Delores held out.

"Do you think she'll want anything to eat?" Richard asked.

Delores spoke up. "I don't think so. She had some canned soup before, and I have chicken soup on the stove for later."

Richard nodded. "I'll tell her it's coming soon. It'll give her something to look forward to." As they turned to go, Molly reminded him, "Don't forget to put on a mask."

"What about you?" he asked as he pulled the masks out of one of the bags.

"I've already been in there. I'll be fine."

He swallowed his argument and followed her upstairs. It only took a couple of minutes to have the humidifier working. It wasn't long before he could tell a difference in his mother's breathing. Though she was still asleep, her breaths were less heavy, less labored. Molly roused her enough to get her to drink some juice, but after half a glass, she went back to sleep.

"Are you sure she's going to be all right?" he asked Molly.

"She'll be fine, Richard. I think the humidifier is already helping her."

"Yes, I agree. I would never have thought of that."

"I'm glad I could help. After all, I feel I owe you and Elizabeth so much for making me feel welcome."

Richard checked himself to keep from saying what came to mind. He'd wanted to say that Molly felt like family, like she belonged. It was an amazing feeling. He hadn't felt like anyone belonged to his family in a long time. Not even his own sister.

But he didn't give voice to those private thoughts.

When they got downstairs, Toby was waiting anxiously for news of his grandmother's condition.

"Toby, your grandmother is doing just fine. The flu makes her want to sleep all the time, but she's doing better, I promise," Molly said, hugging the little boy.

"I'm glad. I don't want Grandma to be sick."

"I know you don't. Why don't we go watch one of the movies Richard bought you?"

After Toby chose *Mary Poppins*, Molly took his hand and they started for the family room.

"I'll come watch it with you," Richard said, following them.

In the family room he settled down with Toby between him and Molly.

The door opened an hour into the video, Delores and Louisa bringing in several dinner trays to them.

"What are you doing, Delores?" Molly asked, stopping the video. "We can come to the table."

"Nonsense. Stay and watch the movie. We won't do this every night, but once in a while will be fun. Right, Toby?"

"Right, Delores," Toby agreed enthusiastically.

"But you have to promise to eat all your food."

"I will. I promise."

"Thanks, Delores," Molly added. "This is nice of you."

After Delores and Louisa had withdrawn, Molly started the movie again, and they ate their soup and warm turkey melt sandwiches.

By the time the movie ended, Toby was curled up between the two adults. "Wasn't that great?" he murmured drowsily.

"Yes, sweetie, it was."

"You want to take him up to bed?" Richard suggested. "I'll take the dishes to the kitchen before I come up."

"Yes, of course. Come along, Toby. It's your bedtime."

"What about Grandma? Won't she want me to hug her good night like I always do?"

"I'm sure she'd like that, but you can't because it might make you sick. When I go in to check on her, I'll tell her that you wanted to. Will that do?"

"I guess so."

Richard grinned at Toby. "It's the best way, Toby. You don't want to be too sick to come down on Christmas morning. That would be a horrible Christmas."

"Yeah, but—but I'm worried about Grandma."

Richard smiled at the little boy. "You're a good boy, Toby. I hope Santa brings you everything you want."

"Thank you, Uncle Richard. I hope the same for you."

Richard stood there, watching Molly lead Toby out of

the den to climb the stairs to bed. Toby was such a sweet boy. Richard realized how much Toby had changed his life. Before Toby and Molly's arrival, he'd worked fifteen-hour days for the past eighteen months. He'd had little interaction with his mother. He'd had no social life.

Now he was spending time with Toby and Molly and his mother. And his life was richer for it. Even after Christmas, he wouldn't work as much as he had been. He'd need to spend time with Toby.

It saddened him to realize how much he'd miss Molly.

He bent and picked up one of the trays and hurried to the kitchen. He didn't want to think about Molly leaving. Not tonight.

Delores protested his actions. She said she and Louisa could've gotten the trays.

"I'll let one of you get the others. I want to get upstairs before Toby goes to sleep. Is that all right?"

"Of course it is. Louisa fed your mom the soup. She didn't quite finish the bowl, but she did a good job."

He thanked Louisa, then made his way upstairs.

"If you and Molly want some coffee and bread pudding, you can come back to the den and I'll bring it in," Delores offered.

"Mmm, we might take you up on that."

Richard sped up the stairs to reach Toby's room just as he was crawling into bed in flannel pajamas.

"Hey, where did you get those pajamas, Toby? I've never seen them."

"Molly bought them for me. She said I'd catch cold wearing just a T-shirt."

"That was thoughtful of her, wasn't it?"

"Yeah. I like them."

Richard got his hug from Toby and watched as Molly received the same. Then they both tiptoed from the room as the boy snuggled under the covers and dozed off.

Molly started down the hallway and Richard caught up with her. But she bypassed the stairs.

"Where are you going?"

"I want to check on your mom."

He passed on what Delores had said, but she still insisted on checking on Elizabeth.

Waiting outside the door for Molly to emerge, he was grateful that Molly was here to monitor his mother's progress.

When she came out, she seemed surprised to find him waiting for her. "Is there something you need?"

"Yes, I need you to come downstairs to have dessert."

"Dessert? Oh, no, I couldn't— What is it?"

"It's Delores's bread pudding, and she makes the best I've ever tasted." He held his hand out to her. "Shall we?"

"I guess so, but it's not good for me to eat dessert every night. I'll have to start working out like you do."

"You can go with me whenever you want. I usually leave around seven." In his mind's eye, he pictured Molly in workout clothes and figured there'd be a riot at the gym with all the men rushing to be next to her.

"I don't think I can while your mother is sick. Toby would be lost if he woke up all alone."

"You're probably right. You're a very thoughtful person, Molly." It felt good to compliment her.

"Thank you. I try to be."

"Did you get money from my mother to pay for the pajamas, by the way?"

"No, I didn't."

Why was she so stubborn about this? He wondered. "Why not? You know, we're supposed to be responsible for Toby now."

"*I* decided to get him the pajamas. It wasn't something he had to have."

"I think it was. From now on, you need to get money from us if you buy Toby something."

Molly, he noticed, stiffened. "What I choose to spend my money on is my business."

Why was she getting upset? He was only looking out for her. "Toby *is* my business and you'll spoil him if you keep on buying him things."

That comment ignited her anger and her eyes sparked as she spat out, "I don't think flannel pajamas will spoil him!"

"Maybe not, but there's no reason for you to pay for them!"

"I think you—"

But Molly never got to finish her thought. Delores came to the hallway and yelled, "What's going on out here?"

CHAPTER TEN

MOLLY FELT like a kid caught with her hand in the proverbial cookie jar. She ducked her head. "Nothing, Delores."

Richard covered up, too. "We were just coming down for the bread pudding."

"Well, come on into the breakfast room. Albert and I thought we'd share it with you, if you don't mind."

"Of course not," Molly immediately said.

Richard kept silent and Molly thought he looked a little irritated, but that was probably because of their argument.

Albert brought in four bowls of bread pudding, while Delores carried a pot of decaf coffee and cups.

"May I get some milk for my coffee, Delores?" Molly asked as she stood.

"Of course. I didn't know you drank milk in your coffee."

"I especially like it late at night."

She felt Richard watching her as she added milk to her coffee. "I'd say she takes coffee in her milk," he commented dryly.

"I can always contribute to the groceries if you want, Richard," she returned coolly.

Delores stared at the two of them. "What is the matter with you two?"

"Sounds like an argument to me," Albert said, keeping his head down and eating his bread pudding.

Richard raked a hand through his hair. "I'm not arguing with Molly, really. But she's been spending her money on Toby's necessities and I think we should be paying the bill. She bought him pajamas."

"Why didn't you ask Richard for the money?" Delores asked her.

"Because I didn't think of it. I've had a lot to deal with."

Delores reached out and patted her hand. "That's true, dear." Then she turned to Richard. "Molly is in a strange city, living with strangers and yet she still manages to know that Toby will need pajamas."

Before Richard could respond, Molly explained, "It's my job to focus on Toby."

"And it's my job to pay for him," Richard retorted sharply. Then he drew a deep breath and let it out, speaking more calmly he said, "That's what I was trying to say earlier, Molly. You see, I've put all the money his parents left him into a trust fund for him. But I expect to pay for the day-to-day things. Not you."

Richard was right.

She hated to admit it, but seeing to the boy's financial needs was a guardian's job, not the nurse's. Why couldn't she see that earlier? Perhaps because she'd come to view Toby as more than a job. She'd come to love the boy.

She saw so much of herself in him, and as such, she wanted to tend to his every need, physical and emotional, the way she'd desperately hoped someone had done for her.

But that was up to Richard now. And Elizabeth.

"I understand, Richard. It won't happen again." She didn't even glance his way, lest he see the anguish in her eyes. Instead, she abruptly changed the subject. "This bread pudding is really good, Delores. What are the chances of prying this recipe out of you too?"

Delores smiled. "When you've got your bags packed and are walking out the door, I'll give you whatever recipes you want, young lady. And not a moment before!"

"You sound like you don't think I'm leaving," Molly said. "I'm due back at the hospital by the fifteenth of January."

"Are you anxious to go back?" Albert asked.

"Yes, and no. I've enjoyed myself here, Albert, getting to do things that I don't do at home. But I love my work."

"I'm just worried because Toby acts like you're his mom. And he's already lost one mom," Albert said with a sigh.

Molly felt like someone had ripped the chair from under her. Is that what Toby thought? Had she been so blinded by her own needs that she couldn't see it? Tears stung her eyes and she fought to keep them back.

Delores elbowed Albert in his side. "He'll be just fine. Don't you worry."

Richard added, "You've always told him that you were going back to Florida. It won't come as a surprise, Molly."

Their words offered her little comfort. Afraid she'd cry in front of everyone, she stood. "I didn't mean to make things worse for Toby. I should never have come here with him." She turned to bolt from the room.

Richard grabbed her arm and stopped her. "No, Molly." He stood up and took her by her shoulders, looking her in the eyes. "You've been wonderful for Toby. Don't you think otherwise." He pulled a handkerchief out of his pocket and wiped the tears from her eyes.

"Toby wouldn't have made it this far as well as he has without you. He still depends on you to help him. But once we get him enrolled in school and he starts making friends, he'll find it easier to tell you goodbye."

Molly looked up at him, her eyes stinging with tears. "Are you sure? I can leave right now if you prefer."

"Absolutely not! Toby would think I drove you away and he'd never forgive me."

"I could wait until morning and explain that I had to go back to the hospital. He'd understand that and he wouldn't blame you, Richard."

"You're staying until mid-January and I don't intend to discuss you leaving early ever again," Richard said emphatically.

He escorted Molly back to her chair. "Now finish your bread pudding before you hurt Delores's feelings."

Though she took a forkful, she couldn't help but search her mind for a way to fix the mistake she'd made.

After a few minutes of idle chitchat, Delores and Albert stood up to say good-night.

"I'm sorry for what I said, Molly," Albert told her. "I couldn't have been more wrong."

Molly smiled at him. "You didn't say anything I shouldn't have realized on my own. Don't worry about it. Good night, Albert."

When the couple left, Richard questioned her. "Do you really think Albert will believe you when your eyes look so sad?"

Molly snapped her head up. "I'm not— My eyes don't look sad!"

"Yes, they do. You can't hide your emotions very well, Molly. Everyone in the house knows how you feel. And they've all fallen in love with your bright smile and warm heart. You're going to have to make a big effort to convince Mom and Toby that you're happy here."

"I am happy here, but I don't want to do irreparable harm to Toby. He's suffered so much already."

"You won't. You've given him a new life and helped him adjust and that's what you need to do when he goes to school, too. He'll want to come home and tell you all about his day."

"Your mother will be here to talk to him."

"Yes, but she's not you. Now, come on up to bed and stop worrying about the future." He led her to the door and then paused.

"Yes? Did you think of something I should do?"

He looked up and then down at her. She automatically looked up and discovered what she'd forgotten.

Mistletoe over the door.

Before she could move away, Richard kissed her.

It wasn't the friendly peck she thought was supposed to happen if you stood under the mistletoe. No, his kiss was skillful and deep and…unlike any kiss she'd ever received.

When he finally raised his head, his gaze fastened on her, she tried to protest, but it didn't come out strong, as she'd intended. "Richard, you—you shouldn't have—"

He took her mouth again, cutting off her protest.

Which was just as well. Truthfully she wanted him to kiss her. Craved his kiss, actually, for a few days now. And she wasn't disappointed.

Richard made her body come alive, and she felt a tingling, a heat, from her head to her toes. No man had ever done that with just a kiss.

Now he looked at her, deeply, staring down into her eyes, his own blue ones smoldering with desire. She recognized the feeling; she felt it, too.

Dangerous, said an inner voice.

Richard was her employer, Toby's guardian, a benefactor to the hospital. She'd best control her desires and remember why she was here.

But his arms were like iron around her, his aftershave like a love potion, drawing her in...

Richard broke the spell he was weaving around her. "We'd better move out of the doorway before I get carried away," he said with a grin, as if his kiss had been a simple Christmas tradition.

As if released from a trance, Molly stammered, "G-good night, Richard." Then she turned and ran up the stairs as if a bogeyman was after her.

But no bogeyman kissed like Richard Anderson.

Molly drew back the curtains, inviting the glorious morning sunshine into the room. Then she woke up her patient. "Good morning, Elizabeth. How are you feeling this morning?"

"Better," Elizabeth said in a small voice.

"I brought up your breakfast. How about sitting on your chair to eat?" Molly put her tray on the coffee table in front of a stone fireplace. Then she built a fire, which seemed to warm the room as much with its orange flame as it did with its heat.

"Delores made you eggs and the apple-walnut muffins you like."

"I do like them," Elizabeth concurred. "Have you tasted them? I'll make you a deal. You try this one and I'll eat the other one." She gave Molly a sly look that made her laugh.

"Good try, Elizabeth." But she took the muffin anyway. Anything to get Elizabeth to eat and regain her strength.

Later when Molly got to the kitchen, she found Richard and Toby eating their breakfasts. Just seeing Richard again stopped her in her tracks. His hair was damp and dark from the shower, and his jaw had a sheen from a clean shave. Memories of their kisses last night assailed her, and she wanted to turn and run again.

As if he read her mind, Richard called out to her. "Come sit down, Molly. We need to get organized for our shopping trip."

Reluctantly Molly joined them at the table.

"I figured Toby and I would shop together first," she said, trying not to make eye contact with him. "After lunch you could take Toby for maybe half an hour. Then we'd be through."

"I don't think so," Richard returned emphatically.

Now she had to look at him. "Why not?"

"I'm going to need several hours with Toby, at least. We've got plans."

Molly's gaze narrowed as Toby and Richard smiled at each other. "I think maybe you've been plotting while I was upstairs."

"Of course. I figured we'd each get two hours with Toby. If we leave here at ten, we'll be at the mall by ten-fifteen. So I'll take him first, since I know the mall, and you can look around. Then we'll meet at twelve-fifteen or twelve-thirty, and have lunch. Then you get him from one to three."

"I'm not sure he'll last that long. He's used to taking a nap, you know," Molly said, smiling at Toby.

"I usually just read a book, Molly. I don't really sleep."

"Fine. But if you get tired, don't blame me!" Molly said.

"Are you mad at me?" Toby asked in concern.

She was mad—but not at Toby. She was mad that she'd have to spend the whole day with Richard. But she couldn't take it out on the boy. "Of course not, Toby. It'll be fun."

"Oh, I promised my mother Toby would visit her this morning, and I need a word with her, too. When should we do that?"

Molly looked at her watch. It was a little after eight now. "Not before nine-thirty, or nine forty-five. Louisa is going to check on her at ten."

"That will be great. Any questions?" Richard asked.

"No, but—your mother gave me this," Molly said, pulling out the envelope. "She said to use it to buy some things for her. I'm a little concerned about carrying around this much cash."

Richard took it from her and opened the envelope. "She asked you to buy some things for her?"

"Yes."

"I can offer to get them for her."

"No, you can't," Molly said, staring at him.

He looked at her until the reason dawned on him. Then he smiled and handed back the envelope. "I see. Well, that will be fine."

Molly shook her head, but she stuffed the envelope back in her jeans pocket.

"I'm going to do some work in my office until nine-thirty. Toby, do you have something you can do? Is there anything on television?"

"I'll go read one of my books. That's more fun."

"I think that's a wise decision. I'll come up and get you when we go to visit Grandma."

"Okay. May I be excused?" he asked.

Molly nodded to him. After all, he'd eaten his breakfast.

It didn't occur to her that she would be alone with Richard again until after Toby ran out the door. Impulsively she stood to take the dishes into the kitchen, hoping Richard would go to his office while she was gone.

When she came back into the breakfast room, he was still sitting there.

"Did you want something else, Richard?"

"No, I'm just moving slowly this morning."

She figured if she moved fast, she could get out of the breakfast room before he realized she was going.

"Well, I won't bother you, then," she said breezily as she rushed past him.

Suddenly, for someone who was moving slowly, he was beside her and caught her in his arms. Then he looked up. "Mistletoe, you know."

And he kissed her again.

CHAPTER ELEVEN

MOLLY couldn't get the kiss out of her mind.

She did the necessary shopping for Elizabeth, buying three gifts for Toby from Santa and the Blackberry for Richard. She had money left over, but she put it in her purse with the receipts from her purchases.

But every moment between purchases, she thought of the kisses Richard had been giving her. She supposed it could be the Christmas spirit filling him, but she didn't think so. She feared he thought she should entertain him at night by giving in to his advances.

Well, he had another thought coming. She certainly wasn't that kind of woman. She was there for Toby, and at the moment, Elizabeth. Not for him to toy with!

Not that she wouldn't want to. Truth be told, she found Richard very attractive. And since she'd been in Dallas, he'd mellowed a lot from the aloof, arrogant man she'd first met in Florida. He was seeming to adapt well to Toby's presence, making every effort to carve a place in his life for the boy. But for her to get involved with Richard would be a mistake. After all, any relationship with him had a definite end point. Mid-January, when she returned to the hospital.

No, she'd just have to control her urges when it came to Richard.

When she met the two males at the appointed place for lunch, she discovered they had made a lot of purchases. "Did you find something for Albert and Delores, and Louisa, too?" she asked.

"Yes, Uncle Richard helped me. And he said to give you back your money."

Richard rolled his eyes. "I told him to do that after we got home. He forgot that part."

"But, Toby, you needed money to buy all the gifts."

"I used Uncle Richard's money. He said it wasn't fair to use yours."

"I see," she said slowly, as Toby put five twenty-dollar bills in her hand. Richard probably couldn't have done anything to make her feel less a part of Toby's family than that. She fought back tears of loneliness. For a little while, she and Toby had been a family. It had been a great feeling.

But now it was gone.

"Molly, is anything wrong?" Richard asked, leaning closer to stare at her face.

"No, absolutely nothing. Let's eat."

Richard had suggested they eat in Neiman Marcus's tearoom. Molly stepped forward and a maître d' led them to a table for four. Once they were seated, Toby needed help with the menu. Molly started to help, but Richard beat her to it. She sat back, realizing Toby turning to Richard was a good thing, she guessed. It would make her departure easier on Toby.

And harder on her.

Richard was already pushing her away so Toby wouldn't be distraught when she left.

When the waitress came to take their orders, Molly asked for a separate check. Richard stared at her. Then he told the waitress to put all three of their lunches on one ticket and bring it to him.

The waitress agreed and Molly sat there in frustration until the woman had walked away. "You've made it clear that I'm not to pay for Toby, but I see no reason not to pay for myself."

"Because you're working for me. I pay for those who work for me."

"I see. So I'm like Delores and Albert? You pay when they go out to eat?"

"I do if they go with me. Don't be difficult, Molly. We want to enjoy our lunch, don't we Toby?"

Molly realized Toby was watching her with a worried frown. "Yes, of course, we do. What did you buy, Toby?"

"I can't tell you!" Toby said.

"Not even what you bought Delores and Albert?"

"Oh, those. Yeah, I got Delores a big bottle of cream of some kind that Uncle Richard said he thought she'd like."

"Oh, that's good. And what did you get Albert?"

"A box of cigars. Uncle Richard said smoking is bad, but Albert likes them and he only smokes them in his apartment."

"I see."

As if he were concerned about what she thought, Richard added, "Toby and I had a long talk about smoking, Molly. I'm sure he understands that he should never do it."

Their food arrived, and all three started to eat.

"What are you and Toby going to shop for after lunch?" Richard asked.

"Oh, odds and ends. I'm not sure since you've taken care of most of the gifts I intended to help him with."

Richard suddenly looked stunned. "I didn't mean to leave you out, Molly. I just wanted to be sure to pay for Toby's shopping. I can give you money if—"

"No, thank you. I have my own money."

That stopped all conversation. They ate in silence until they were finished.

"Did you like your lunch, Toby?"

"Yeah, but this is kind of a fancy place, isn't it?"

Molly smiled. "I doubt that your uncle would've chosen it if I hadn't come with you. This is a tearoom and usually just women come here to eat."

"Oh. I understand." He turned to Richard. "It's like when we went to the movie that Molly and Grandma liked."

Richard smiled. "That's right, Toby."

"Hey, Molly, did you see Santa Claus? I got my picture taken with him. Wanna see it?"

So Richard couldn't have waited for her to see Toby with Santa? Almost of their own will, her eyes sought his and she glared at him, at the same time she said sweetly to Toby, "Of course I do, Toby. Was it fun?"

"Yeah. I learned the truth about Santa last year in school, but I still like to pretend."

"I understand." She took the picture Toby handed her. "Oh, I like this picture. I'm so glad your uncle Richard had this taken. We'll need to get a frame for it."

"We got one already. I need to put it in there before it gets all bent."

"Yes. Maybe your uncle Richard will help you," Molly said pointedly and then felt ashamed of herself.

"No, I saved that job for you, Molly. I'm not very good at that." Richard smiled at her.

"I see. Of course I'll help you, Toby. Where's the frame?"

Toby bent over and pulled a nice frame out of his bag. Molly had the picture in place in a couple of minutes. Then she held it up for Toby and Richard to see. "How does it look?"

"Perfect," Richard said. "You want to go get your picture taken on Santa's knee?"

Molly was surprised by a wave of sadness. "No, it's only for children."

Her sadness must have shown on her face, because Richard asked, "Molly, are you all right?"

She nodded and lowered her gaze. "It's just…well, foster children didn't get to go to the mall and see Santa."

"Why not?" Toby asked.

"Because we knew he wasn't going to bring us what we asked for. We usually got a new pair of socks and a little doll for the girls and a truck or car for the boys."

"That's all?" Toby asked in horror.

"Toby, let's not talk about sad things," Richard said. "We want this Christmas to be a happy one for Molly, don't we?"

"Yes, we do. And we bought you some presents, Molly!" Then Toby clapped his hands over his mouth. "But I can't tell you."

Richard laughed. "Remind me not to tell you any more secrets, Toby, my boy!"

"Sorry, Uncle Richard. But I didn't tell her what they are."

"That's true. Okay, I'll forgive you."

"Phew, I'm glad."

"It's time for our shopping to begin, Toby," Molly said. "Are you ready to go?"

"I'm carrying some things to the car," Richard said before they could move. "Want me to take your bags, too, Molly? I'll promise not to peek in them."

"Are you sure?" Molly asked, trying to smile.

"I cross my heart, honey. No peeking."

"Okay," she agreed, wanting to leave him as soon as she could. He may not peek into the bags but he'd already pried into her heart. And she wanted to keep her feelings hidden.

After Richard took their packages, Molly and Toby went shopping. Toby wanted to get his uncle what Molly had chosen for Albert, a pocketknife. Molly steered him into a smaller version, more gentlemanly, that wouldn't be a bulge in Richard's expensive suits.

Molly had already bought Richard a mystery novel she hoped he'd make time to read now. She also bought him a DVD of a mystery movie she'd seen last year and liked.

By the time they met Richard, they had quite a few packages. She asked if they could stop at a store so she could buy wrapping paper and ribbon to make bows.

"You didn't have yours gift-wrapped?" Richard asked in surprise.

"I usually do the wrapping myself."

"I see. Of course. There's a store right over here that carries wrapping stuff."

"I won't be a moment if you and Toby want to wait in the car."

After Molly rushed into the store, Richard said, "You didn't tell her what we bought for her, did you?"

"No, I promise, Uncle Richard."

Molly came back to the car with a big package. "Do you have enough patience for me to get one more thing?"

"Sure," Richard said. "Where do you want to go?"

"It's right here. I'll hurry."

Richard saw that she was watching Toby. He turned to the little boy. "While Molly is doing more shopping, why don't you lie down in the back seat and rest. It's been a long day, hasn't it."

Toby seemed willing to rest a little. Molly nodded at Richard and hurried into another store. When she came out she had a large package in a plastic bag. She opened the back of the vehicle and stuck it in.

As she got in the truck, she saw Toby asleep on the back seat.

"Oh, good," she said with a sigh.

"You'd better hope he doesn't wake up. Once he smells that last purchase, it'll be hard to keep him away from it."

Molly nodded. "I know. I'm ready to eat it all now."

"We'll have plenty to eat on Christmas Day. Why did you buy that?"

"I always buy a small bag of caramel corn, but this year I'm sharing the holiday with all of you, so I thought I should get enough for all of us." She remembered caramel corn being a part of Christmas when she was a child; her parents always had some in her stocking on Christmas morning.

"I'm going to hide it until Christmas Eve after Toby has gone to bed."

"You'd better hope he can't smell it."

"I know."

When they got home, Richard carried Toby up to his room. The little boy didn't even wake up.

Then he came back down to help carry up the packages. Molly had sorted out her packages and left his alone.

"I didn't want to be accused of peeking," she said.

"Wouldn't matter because all mine are already wrapped."

"And you certainly have a lot."

"Yes, I'm a real Santa Claus," he said with a grin. It reminded Molly of how he looked just before he kissed her. She backed away.

"Well, I'll take my packages to my room so I can wrap them."

"Okay, I'll put mine under the tree."

Molly went up the stairs, forcing herself not to run to the garden room where the tree stood. She loved the idea of a big tree with lots of beautiful presents under it. But she'd sneak a peek later this evening. Alone.

The rest of the week sped by. One day they baked sugar cookies and decorated them with colored icing. To Molly's surprise, Richard joined them in the kitchen and then the breakfast room where they sat down to do the decorating.

They had a lot of fun. Richard teased Toby about his artistic efforts, but Molly teased Richard, telling him Toby was better at decorating than he was. They both agreed that Molly was better than either of them, and she assured them it was because she'd had lots of practice.

"You got to decorate cookies when you were a foster child?" Toby asked.

"No, but I usually bake cookies and decorate them to give to friends and people in the hospital."

"That's really nice, Molly," Richard said.

"Should we give some of our cookies to people in the hospital?" Toby asked.

"We could, Toby. But I'm not sure we'll have enough. Maybe we could just take cookies to the children's ward of a nearby hospital."

"That would be Presbyterian. I'll call and see how many kids they have in the hospital over Christmas. I bet it's not too many."

Richard checked and said they only had fourteen children who would be there a few days.

So the next morning, they took bags of cookies, some extra for the nurses on duty, and passed them out to the children in the hospital. Toby met and visited with another boy his age.

When they left the hospital, Toby hugged Richard and told him how lucky he was to have his uncle and grandmother.

Elizabeth was doing much better, getting a little stronger each day. But when they planned their horse and buggy ride to see the Christmas lights, she decided to pass.

It wasn't a terribly cold night, but the blanket the driver covered them with was welcome. Molly insisted Toby sit between her and Richard, so he wouldn't fall out. Both males looked at her like she was crazy, but she held her position. Mainly because she didn't want to sit next to Richard. She was afraid the evening would be too romantic, and she might succumb to the idea of snuggling up next to Richard.

Many of the residents of Highland Park had great light displays and the buggy moved slowly past them, giving Toby plenty of time to examine each one and pick his favorite. On the way home, he asked Richard about having a light display of their own next year.

Molly told herself she was pleased that Toby could think of the future without pain. He had made remarkable strides in the two weeks he'd been in Dallas. But she wouldn't be there next year to see their lights. And that made her sad.

"What do you think, Molly?"

"About what?" she asked in surprise.

"See, Toby, she wasn't listening. We were talking about the lights we should have next year. Do you have an opinion?"

"I can't decide whether I like the multicolored ones or the white lights. What do you think, Toby?"

"I like all the colored lights. But the white lights that had deer grazing on their lawns did look nice."

"Well, maybe we will try some lights next year. I'll have to contact one of the lighting companies that does the displays in March or April and let them bring some suggestions for us to choose from."

"You mean they don't do the lights themselves?" Toby asked, disappointment in his voice.

"I think it might take too long on a house as big as yours, Toby," Molly explained.

"Yeah, or the dad might fall and break his neck," Richard said. "I haven't forgotten who had to climb up so high just to put the angel on the Christmas tree!"

"But you did a great job," Toby said with a grin.

Once they got home, Toby rushed upstairs to tell Elizabeth all about what they'd seen. Which left Molly alone with Richard.

"Thank you, Richard. That was fun."

"Yes, it was, wasn't it? But I would've had more fun if you'd let Toby sit on the side and you sat next to me."

"I don't see that that would've made a difference."

"I could've cuddled with you under the blanket. Toby was so busy jumping up to see everything, he kept letting in the cold air."

"You survived."

"I did, but I would've had more fun the other way." He winked at her.

"Richard, you shouldn't—"

He pulled her against him and kissed her again. She'd told herself she'd hate it if he kissed her again, but she'd known she was lying. When his warm lips touched hers, she melted in his embrace and her arms reached up around his neck.

When he finally pulled away, she drew a deep breath. "I don't think we should do that anymore. There's no mistletoe here and your mother would be very upset if she saw us kissing."

"Do you think so?"

"Yes, of course. And Delores could've walked in on us at any time!"

"And you think she'd be upset, too?" He was smiling, with a glint in his eyes that worried her.

"I—I have to go upstairs," she said and hurried away.

Richard watched Molly's trim figure run up the stairs… away from him.

He thought she liked his kisses, because she didn't pull away. He hoped she liked them. As each day passed, he was realizing he needed Molly in his life. The past eighteen months had been horrible. At lot of the time he'd put in at the law firm had been necessary, but he was coming to realize that some of it had been because life had changed and he didn't know how to deal with it.

With Molly in his life, he didn't need to hide anymore.

She brought joy to his days. He loved having breakfast with her each morning, and all the Christmas activities were more fun with her along.

Of course, Toby was part of the fun, too.

He'd often thought he would one day marry and have children, but somehow that kept getting pushed back to some distant time in the future. Now he had Toby, a son, to raise. And, for a while, he had Molly.

He already had put some plans in place to try to convince Molly to stay. But he wasn't sure what her reaction would be. With a hopeful heart, he tried not to think she would turn him down.

When his mother started coming down for dinner again, they moved back to the dining room for that meal. Toby, no longer shy, talked a blue streak, telling Elizabeth about the things they'd done while she was ill. He talked a lot about their trip to the hospital.

"I think that was a wonderful thing you did, Molly, suggesting you take some cookies to the hospital."

"Thank you, Elizabeth, but it was Richard who checked with the hospital and got an okay for us doing that."

"Then, Richard, you deserve some praise, too. I think that it's time I go back to doing my charity work. And we should plan to make it a Christmas tradition to bring cookies to the hospital."

"I agree, Mom," Richard said. "By the way, have you eaten any of the cookies we made?"

"No, I haven't even seen them. Does Delores have them in the kitchen?"

"Yes, she's going to serve them for dessert tonight," Richard said. It was Saturday night before Christmas on

Monday. "She wanted you to have some now that you're not sick."

"Oh, that's a delightful idea. You must've made a lot of cookies," Elizabeth said.

"It took us two days to decorate all of them."

"Yeah, I pooped out, Grandma. I just watched them while I ate a couple of cookies," Toby said with a grin. "Uncle Richard said I was being lazy, but I told him I'd lost my artistic drive," Toby said in precise words, grinning at his uncle.

"What a con artist you are, Toby! You just decided you wanted to eat the cookies more than you wanted to decorate them," Richard retorted.

"I put the little silver balls on the stars you decorated!" Toby said. "That was decorating, too, wasn't it, Molly?

"Yes, sweetheart, it was. And there were a lot of cookies to decorate."

Delores, who entered the room in the middle of the discussion, carrying a plate of decorated cookies, said, "And maybe you would've been as inspired if you'd had a girl to kiss under the mistletoe like your uncle did."

Since Molly and Richard both turned red in the cheeks, no one had to ask who was doing the kissing.

CHAPTER TWELVE

"DOES that mean you're going to stay, Molly?" Toby asked, his eyes wide with contained excitement.

She shook her head. But before she could say anything, Richard spoke up. "I'll explain later, Toby." She wanted to hear his explanation. Exactly why was Richard kissing her under the mistletoe? Was it only because of tradition...or did he actually have feelings for her?

After dinner Richard took Toby aside for a man-to-man talk, none of which she could hear without being obvious. He must have explained himself well, though, because Toby didn't ask any more questions all night. Nor did Elizabeth, who was strangely quiet.

Even on Sunday, Christmas Eve, at services, Elizabeth didn't maneuver them together in the pew. They ended up together naturally.

"I love to go to church at Christmas time," Molly said as they were seated in a restaurant for lunch after services. "All the carols. Your church has a talented choir, Elizabeth."

"Yes, we do. And the decorations are beautiful. Especially the manger scene." Elizabeth referred to the living nativity, complete with real animals.

From the back seat Toby chimed in. "I liked the donkey. He kept eating all the hay."

"I'm sure they'll get more," Richard said. "I think you liked him because he looked like a big dog."

"Yeah," Toby admitted, grinning. "But my Sunday School teacher told us a story about a dog that was neat."

"I enjoyed Sunday School this morning, too," Richard said, his gaze on Molly. They had both gone to the Singles class together.

"What did you think, Molly?" Elizabeth asked.

Before she could answer, Richard said, "She thought she was surrounded by hungry dogs!"

"You had dogs in your class?" Toby asked with envy.

"No, sweetie," Molly hurriedly assured him. "Richard was referring to some gentlemen in the class who were…very welcoming."

"Yes," Richard said. "They all wanted to ask Molly out."

Toby looked shocked. Fortunately their meals, that they'd previously ordered, appeared at the table and gained the boy's attention.

Molly, however, noted Elizabeth's amused look.

In truth, Molly had been glad Richard had taken such proprietary interest in her. She was a little too shy for such determined interest as the men had shown. It would make her reluctant to attend that class again without Richard.

They met in the family room later on and watched the DVD of *It's a Wonderful Life*, having talked about the movie over lunch. They'd promised Toby they'd show him the holiday classic. He delighted when Clarence got his wings and declared his parents had become angels, too.

After dinner, they all went into the garden room and Richard turned on the Christmas lights. In the darkness they glowed softly, creating an atmosphere of magic.

Toby sighed. "Isn't it wonderful?"

"The lights, you mean, and the tree?" Molly asked. After he nodded his head, she said, "Yes, more beautiful than any I've ever seen, Toby."

"I think so, too," Toby agreed.

Richard and Elizabeth agreed, Elizabeth pointing out that Toby had chosen all the ornaments, so he should take pride in the tree.

Finally Molly told Toby it was time to go to bed, so Santa could come visit their house. He agreed and gave his normal hugs to Richard and Elizabeth.

Upstairs, he got in his flannel pajamas and knelt down by his bed to say his prayers, as he'd done every night in Dallas. Molly sat on the edge of his bed, waiting. But when he said nothing, Molly looked down at Toby. "Is something wrong, sweetheart?"

Toby lowered his head for a moment. Then he said, "Molly, do you think Mommy and Daddy will be upset that I'm happy?"

Molly's throat tightened for a moment and she fought the tears that filled her eyes. Then she reached down and lifted Toby into her lap. "No, baby, I think they'll be happy that you're happy. That's what they want. That's what every mommy and daddy want for their children."

"I've been worrying about that. I love living here with Uncle Richard and Grandma, and you, too. But I wish my mommy and daddy were here with us."

"Of course you do. They know you haven't forgotten

them, Toby. I told you they were in your heart. That means they know what you're thinking and feeling. It's okay to be happy."

Toby hugged her tightly. "Thank you. I knew you would know."

He kissed her on the cheek and then climbed into bed. "I love you, Molly."

"I love you, too, Toby."

She tucked him into bed and tiptoed out of his room. As she got to the stairway, on her way down to see if the coast was clear for her to take down her gifts, she ran into Elizabeth on her way up.

"Are you going to bed now?" Molly asked.

"Yes. We'll be getting up early in the morning. Richard said to tell you no one is to come downstairs until seven. I think he told Toby he should wake you up before he comes down.

"Yes, he did. I'll keep Toby up here until seven. Then we'll all go down together?"

"Yes, so we can all see Toby's reaction."

"Fine. Well, I hope you get a good night's sleep."

"I will. And you, too." Elizabeth smiled and then continued to her bedroom.

When Molly got downstairs, she didn't find Richard anywhere. She went to the kitchen to ask where he was.

"He said he had to run an errand," Delores said. "Albert and I were about to have a cup of decaf. Want to join us?"

"Yes, please, and thank you for asking. Are we having Christmas cookies, too?"

"I was afraid everyone would be tired of them."

"How could we be? It's like pure sugar," Molly said with a laugh.

They were enjoying their snack, chatting about their day, when they heard the side door open.

"Is that Richard?" Molly asked.

"I'll go check," Albert said, jumping up and running out of the room before anyone could call out.

Molly sat there for a minute before she asked Delores, "Did that seem odd to you?"

"Yes, it did. I wonder what those two are up to."

Only a minute later, Richard stuck his head in the door. "I'm going on up to bed. We've got to get up early in the morning. Good night."

Only after Richard had left the room did Albert reappear.

"Is everything okay?" Delores asked him.

"Uh, yeah, fine."

Shortly afterward, Molly went up to gather her gifts and take them downstairs in a big shopping bag. By the time she'd added them, the pile under the Christmas tree was ridiculously huge. But she stood there, staring at the big tree and all the presents, wanting to remember this very special Christmas. Would she ever have another one like it?

Richard was up long before seven o'clock. His roommate had insisted on getting out of bed at five-thirty. Of course, he should've been grateful, since the puppy promptly relieved himself on the throw rug by his bed.

"Thanks, you rotten little puppy. I'll be glad when you have a name, so I can chew you out properly."

Of course, he was already attached to the animal. He'd intended for it to sleep in a box in the corner of his room, but an hour of listening to the puppy's cries was enough to convince him to take the dog into his bed.

That warm little body curled up against his chest was unbelievably comforting. He had in mind a different bed partner in the future, but the puppy would do for now.

He talked the dog into another hour in bed before he got up and went downstairs, the puppy carried in his arms. He had a box prepared, wrapped in Christmas paper with holes poked through the cardboard and wrapping paper so the puppy could breathe, but he didn't want to put the dog in it until the last minute.

In the meantime, he wrote a letter from Santa to Toby and attached it to the bag of dog food sitting right in front of the tree, where it wouldn't be missed.

When he heard some stirring around upstairs, he hurriedly put the puppy in the box, placed the lid on it and moved to the foot of the staircase.

There was Molly, her reddish curls tumbling about her shoulders, dressed in jeans and a sweater, holding Toby's hand. He'd gotten dressed, too. Elizabeth was wearing a robe, looking comfortable and warm.

"I came down to turn on the Christmas lights," Richard called up the stairs. "Are you ready to see if Santa came to see us?"

Toby didn't wait until he finished. He was downstairs before the other two even started down.

"Steady, there, Toby. We have to wait for the ladies, you know."

"But you saw the tree. Did Santa come?"

"You know, I think he did, but I just glanced at the tree. I didn't want to spoil the surprise."

When the ladies reached them, Toby again took Molly's hand. Richard escorted his mother in first, followed by Molly and Toby. Elizabeth sat down in a chair, clearing Toby's sight to the tree. The first thing he saw was the letter from Santa to him.

"Santa left me a letter?" he asked. He pulled it from the sack it was attached to, not noticing what the sack was. Molly did notice, and Richard watched as her eyes widened.

Toby read the note. "I think Santa got me confused with another Toby. He thinks I have a dog."

Just then, they all heard squeaking.

Richard, to hurry the discovery along, because the suspense was killing him, said, "I think that box is making noises. Maybe you'd better open it quickly, Toby."

Toby looked at his uncle and then at Molly. Slowly he fell to his knees and reached out to take off the lid, his fingers shaking. The minute the lid came off, the excited puppy came up on his hind legs, trying to climb out of the box, his tail wagging frantically.

"Molly, look! It's a puppy! It's really a puppy!"

Richard saw the tears in Toby's eyes as he picked up the dog and hugged it to him. When Richard looked at Molly, he saw tears streaming down her face, too.

"Can I keep him, Uncle Richard? Is he really mine?"

"He really is, Toby. You get to name him and everything." While he talked, Richard moved to Molly's side and put his arms around her. He knew she was happy for Toby, but he hadn't expected it to make her cry.

She lay her head on his shoulder and he pulled a handkerchief out of his pocket to mop up her tears again.

"Molly, what can I name him?" Toby asked her.

"Whatever you like. I think he's a chocolate Lab."

"Chocolate? Oh, I know! I'll name him Cocoa, like the drink."

"That's a great name for him, Toby," Richard said. "And look, his leash is attached, so you can take him outside when you need to."

"How will I know?"

"You'll learn the signs, Toby, after you've cleaned up the messes he makes."

"Do you think he needs to go now?"

"No, I'm, uh, sure Santa took him before he left him behind."

"Oh. Uncle Richard, thank you for my puppy," Toby said, reaching up to hug Richard's neck. Richard had to bend down to his level but he straightened in a hurry, afraid Molly would move away from him.

Toby ran to his grandmother, too. "Thank you, Grandma! For a minute, I thought maybe Daddy and Mommy had told Santa. But then I remembered that Santa isn't real."

"He's real in our hearts, child," Elizabeth said.

"That's what Molly said about Mommy and Daddy, that they were in my heart."

"That's true," Elizabeth said softly, blinking rapidly.

"How about we open some presents?" Richard said. "Let me see if Albert and Delores are ready to come in." Before he left Molly, he dropped a kiss on her lips.

When Delores and Albert came in, Toby immediately showed them Cocoa. Then he asked Albert how he knew if Cocoa had to go outside. They had a brief discussion in lowered voices.

Richard picked up a package for Albert and asked Toby to carry it to him. Toby had to put his puppy in Molly's lap to do so. Then he carried a package to his grandmother. Molly played with the puppy, loving its silky warmth. In a minute, Richard bent down to her on the sofa and whispered, "Do I need to get you a puppy, too?"

"Oh, no! I mean, he's sweet, but I have to work and he'd be lonesome.

"A bike!" Toby suddenly shouted.

The tree had hidden the bike on the far side.

"Is it for me?" he asked hesitantly, as if afraid to hope.

"I don't know. It looks a little small for me, but it could be for Molly," Richard said.

Toby rolled the bike over to Molly, his face serious. "Do you think it's for you, Molly?"

"No, sweetheart. Your Uncle Richard is teasing you. The bike is for you."

"Wow! That's almost as good as Cocoa!"

"But you can only ride it in the backyard unless someone is with you, Toby. You must promise to obey that rule." Richard gave him a stern look.

"I will, I promise. In the backyard Cocoa can run along beside me!"

"True," Richard said with a smile. "I think I might as well pass out the other gifts. Toby seems too occupied with the two he's gotten so far."

Molly still held Cocoa while Toby fiddled with his bike, examining every inch of it. Elizabeth had a small gift she was opening, and Molly realized it was one she'd had made for her. She held her breath, hoping she'd made the right decision.

Suddenly Elizabeth burst into tears.

"I'm sorry, Elizabeth. I thought you'd— I can take it—"

Elizabeth clutched it to her breast. "No, I love it! I'm sorry I cried, but I wasn't prepared— It's wonderful!"

"What is it, Mom?" Richard asked, kneeling beside his mother.

Elizabeth held out a small jeweled frame with a picture of her daughter, Susan.

"That's Mommy!" Toby exclaimed.

"I know, sweetheart." She wiped the tears. "The pictures I have of her are as a little girl. Her father wouldn't let me keep any recent pictures of her."

Richard kissed his mother's cheek. Then he moved over and kissed Molly on the lips, taking her by surprise.

"That was very sweet of you, Molly."

"Thank you, but— Thank you. I, uh, borrowed Toby's small picture of him and his parents, and the photo shop was able to take her out and make a picture of just her."

"You cut up my picture?" Toby asked in horror.

"No, sweetheart, I would never do that. They can make a new picture without cutting up yours."

Richard unwrapped his book from her. "I've been wanting to read this. I've decided to slow down and enjoy life more. This will help me do that."

Albert was very proud of the pocketknife Molly had bought him. "I lost my last one and I've been planning to buy another, but I haven't. This is perfect."

Delores sighed when she opened her box of chocolates. "I can't wait to eat them," she said to Molly. "Thank you."

Toby had lots of presents, some from Molly, some marked from Santa. He received games and books, including *Charlotte's Web*. "Hey, look, Molly, now we can read a chapter every night!"

"Yes, sweetie, we can."

Then he unwrapped another gift from Molly. It was a frame with the picture of him and his parents enlarged to an 8 x 10. "Thank you, Molly!"

Molly had received some good-smelling perfume from Toby and a necklace and earrings from Elizabeth. They were beautiful cubic zirconia but glistened like real diamonds. Next Richard handed her a big box that intrigued her. She couldn't imagine anything that size.

When she opened the box, she stared at the contents, completely surprised. A bejeweled top in dark green with colored stones and gold ribbon all over it. Beneath that was a lush velvet floor-length skirt in the same dark green. She couldn't take her eyes off the outfit. It made her think of Cinderella, except that she, Molly, had no ball to attend.

She looked up to find Richard smiling at her.

"Is this from you?" she asked in surprise.

"Actually it's a second gift from Mom, but I picked it out."

"You did? It's beautiful…in fact, it's incredible. But I don't go anywhere I could wear it, Elizabeth, so maybe you should return it."

Elizabeth looked at her son. "That's your cue, Richard."

"I have to go to a New Year's Eve party, Molly. I was hoping you'd agree to go with me."

"Oh, no! I—I couldn't. I'm sure you have someone else to ask, Richard."

"No, I don't. I could find someone else, but she wouldn't be the woman of my heart, like you are."

Molly stared at him, speechless. What was he saying?

"I think you should take her to another room where you'll have some privacy, Richard," Elizabeth said, nudging her son.

Molly had no idea what was going on, and no time to figure it out. Richard tugged on her hands and she rose, handing Toby the puppy.

When they got to the family room, Richard didn't let her sit down. Instead he gathered her in his arms. "Is it a complete surprise, Molly?"

Was what a complete surprise? Molly still didn't follow. Or maybe, she realized, she was getting her Christmas wish. She looked up into Richard's blue eyes, alit by the morning sunlight streaming through the windows. Did she dare hope…?

He smiled at her then, and she knew. He loved her.

"But, Richard, I'm a nurse and I work long hours— in Florida!"

"I hope not. Not the nurse part, but definitely the Florida part. You can get a job here if you want, but not until you marry me. And then I think we should have children so Toby won't be spoiled rotten by you and Mom."

"You—you want to marry me?" Molly asked, wonder in her voice.

"I know we didn't start off too well, but once I got to know you, I haven't been able to resist you. I couldn't figure out a way to change our relationship except by kissing you. And you seemed resistant to that."

He should only know how much she'd wanted that kiss. "Not too resistant since you didn't stop."

"Oh, I haven't begun to kiss you yet, Molly Soderling soon-to-be Anderson. You will marry me, won't you?"

She yearned to say yes, but doubt still lingered in her pragmatic mind. "Are you sure we're compatible?"

He kissed her, one of those long, sweet kisses she loved. Then he whispered, "We are compatible, aren't we?"

"I—I think so. You're not just doing this because Toby wants me to stay?"

Richard chuckled. "I love Toby, but I don't think I'd ask a woman to marry me just to please him."

"Your mother likes me, too."

"That's handy, since she's going to be your mother-in-law."

"I hadn't thought of that! Oh, Richard, I'm so lucky."

"Now I'm jealous of my mother."

"Don't be. You're the one I want to spend my life with. But your mother and Toby make it even more special." Tears glistened in her eyes as she gazed at him. "I've always been alone. I was dreading leaving because I would miss everyone so much."

"And I couldn't stand the thought of you leaving, either."

"Now I'll never have to leave."

"And you'll always have wonderful Christmases."

"And most of all, I'll always have you," she said softly before she kissed him.

For the first time she surrendered to his kiss. It was the best kiss of all.

EPILOGUE

RICHARD was talking with Toby while he waited for Molly to come down. It was New Year's Eve and he was escorting Molly to the party he'd mentioned on Christmas Day.

A noise alerted him and he turned to stare up the stairs where Molly stood.

Now he knew how Cinderella's prince felt. Only he was the lucky one. His Cinderella was coming toward him, not running away.

The dress he'd picked out looked even better on her. It picked up the green in her eyes and made her hair look more auburn than brown. She looked gorgeous.

Her hair was done in a French pleat and she was wearing the necklace and earrings Elizabeth had given her for Christmas, too. She'd bought gold sandal heels and her nails had been painted a dark red. Every inch of her was perfect.

He met her at the bottom of the stairs. "You look wonderful," he whispered and kissed her.

"Don't mess up her lipstick, Richard!" Elizabeth scolded him. "I thought I had taught you better than that."

"Sorry, Mom. I'll let her apply more lipstick before we get out of the car."

"Doesn't she look splendid?"

"Absolutely," he returned and added another kiss.

"Does splendid mean pretty?" Toby asked. "'Cause I think Molly looks pretty."

"You're right, Toby," Richard said and kissed her again.

"No more compliments, Toby, or she won't have any lipstick on when they get to the party," Elizabeth warned. "Run along now, and have a good time."

Once they were in Richard's vehicle, Molly wrapped in his mother's black mink coat, she said, "I really do feel like Cinderella at the ball. Do I have to be home by midnight?"

"Probably, because that's the only way I'll be able to keep you to myself," Richard said. "By the way, I forgot to tell you on Christmas, but the jewelry my mom got you—"

"I know. I'm wearing them."

"I don't think you know this. They're real."

Molly stared at him, processing his words. "But that would mean…It's a diamond necklace! No, Richard, that can't be true!"

"It is. Mom wanted you to have your own necklace and earrings as a starter set. She's big on jewelry."

"But I can't wear real diamonds! I might lose them!"

"Don't say that or I can't give you your New Year's present."

Molly looked even more stunned. "A New Year's present? But I don't have one for you."

"Yes, you do. You just don't realize it yet."

He pulled over to the side of the road and parked.

Molly looked out the window. "Are we here already?"

"No. But I can't drive and give you your gift at the same time."

"But it's not New Year's yet."

"I want you to have this before we go into the party. Like a This Property Is Taken kind of sign."

She stared at him, having no idea what he was talking about.

Then he opened a small box he pulled from the breast pocket of his coat. "Are you sure you can't wear just one more diamond?"

She stared at the ring in the box, the size of the diamond stunning her. "It's huge! Richard—"

He kissed her several times before he allowed her to speak again. "Now, say yes."

"Yes," she said obediently. She knew what she was saying yes to and she had no hesitation.

He slid the ring on her finger. It was a perfect fit. "How did you know my size?"

"Mom guessed it when she was having you try on her rings."

"I hadn't thought of that."

"And will you wear the ring tonight?"

She smiled at him. "Of course. I don't want anyone thinking you're free."

He laughed. "Me, neither."

"Richard, when will we get married?"

"If I had a choice, it would be tomorrow."

"On New Year's Day? Aren't you supposed to be watching football all day?"

"I'd rather be marrying you, but I'm willing to wait until the first weekend in February. Mom says she thinks she can call in some favors and have it arranged by then. Will that be all right with you?"

"It sounds perfect."

"Give Mom the names of any of your friends from Florida and she'll send the invitations. Then call them and if they can come, I'll buy the plane tickets for them."

She threw her arms around his neck. "Richard, you never cease to amaze me. You are the most thoughtful man I've ever met."

"That's because I'm the luckiest man you've ever met. Getting to marry you is something I'll always be grateful for."

"I love you so much," she whispered as she got rid of the last of her lipstick in the best way possible.

At a late breakfast on New Year's Day, Molly showed her ring to Toby and Elizabeth.

"Oh, it's beautiful," Elizabeth said, a big smile on her face.

"Thank you, Elizabeth," Molly returned and kissed Elizabeth's cheek.

Toby watched them. Then Delores and Albert came in and congratulated Richard and Molly. After a couple of minutes of silence, Toby said, "Uncle Richard, how come Molly's the only one who got something for New Year's?"

"Well, it's not because it's New Year's, Toby. It's because we got engaged."

Toby sat silently for a few seconds and then his eyes grew large. "You mean you're going to marry Molly? And she'll stay with us forever and ever?"

Richard grinned. "That's exactly what I mean. Pretty cool, huh?"

"Oh, yeah!" He got up and hugged Molly's neck. "I'm so glad you're going to stay."

Molly hugged him tightly. "Me, too."

He sat back down in his chair and took a bite of his eggs and chewed them slowly. Then he looked at Richard again. "Does that mean you'll have some kids?"

"Hopefully, but we've already got one child to raise."

Toby sat there thinking about that. Suddenly he raised his head and looked at Richard. "Do you mean me?"

"Of course I do, Toby. I know you'll always love your mommy and daddy, but they can't be here, so Molly and I will be your new mommy and daddy."

"You will? And I can call you my mommy and daddy when I go to school, so I'll be like the other kids?"

"Yes, you can, Toby," Molly promised, a loving smile on her face. She hugged Toby and Richard did, too.

Toby looked at Elizabeth. "Isn't this neat, Grandma?"

"Yes, it is, Toby. We're so lucky to have a family like ours. We must never forget how lucky we are."

"No, I won't forget," Toby said soberly.

"Go get your coat, son," Richard said. "Albert and I are going to play football with you."

Joy broke across Toby's face and he ran from the room.

Richard kissed Molly goodbye and grabbed his coat, calling over his shoulder, "That was a good breakfast, Delores. Albert, are you ready?"

Toby came running to join them and the three males went to the backyard.

Molly leaned toward Elizabeth. "Life never stops, does it?"

"Thank goodness, no. It just keeps going. Just like our family."

* * * * *

New York Times *bestselling author Linda Lael Miller is back with a new romance featuring the heartwarming McKettrick family from Silhouette Special Edition.*

SIERRA'S HOMECOMING
by Linda Lael Miller

On sale December 2006,
wherever books are sold.

Turn the page for a sneak preview!

Soft, smoky music poured into the room.

The next thing she knew, Sierra was in Travis's arms, close against that chest she'd admired earlier, and they were slow dancing.

Why didn't she pull away?

"Relax," he said. His breath was warm in her hair.

She giggled, more nervous than amused. What was the matter with her? She was attracted to Travis, had been from the first, and he was clearly attracted to her. They were both adults. Why not enjoy a little slow dancing in a ranch-house kitchen?

Because slow dancing led to other things. She took a step back and felt the counter flush against her lower back. Travis naturally came with her, since they were holding hands and he had one arm around her waist.

Simple physics.

Then he kissed her.

Physics again—this time, not so simple.

"Yikes," she said, when their mouths parted.

He grinned. "Nobody's ever said that after I kissed them."

She felt the heat and substance of his body pressed

against hers. "It's going to happen, isn't it?" she heard herself whisper.

"Yep," Travis answered.

"But not tonight," Sierra said on a sigh.

"Probably not," Travis agreed.

"When, then?"

He chuckled, gave her a slow, nibbling kiss. "Tomorrow morning," he said. "After you drop Liam off at school."

"Isn't that…a little…soon?"

"Not soon enough," Travis answered, his voice husky. "Not nearly soon enough."

nocturne™

**Explore the dark and sensual
new realm of paranormal romance.**

HAUNTED
BY LISA CHILDS

**The first book in the riveting
new 3-book miniseries, Witch Hunt.**

DEATH CALLS
BY CARIDAD PIÑEIRO

**Darkness calls to humans,
as well as vampires...**

*On sale December 2006,
wherever books are sold.*

REQUEST YOUR FREE BOOKS!
2 FREE NOVELS PLUS 2
FREE GIFTS!

HARLEQUIN ROMANCE

From the Heart, For the Heart

YES! Please send me 2 FREE Harlequin Romance® novels and my 2 FREE gifts. After receiving them, if I don't wish to receive any more books, I can return the shipping statement marked "cancel." If I don't cancel, I will receive 4 brand-new novels every month and be billed just $3.57 per book in the U.S., or $4.05 per book in Canada, plus 25¢ shipping and handling per book and applicable taxes, if any*. That's a savings of over 15% off the cover price! I understand that accepting the 2 free books and gifts places me under no obligation to buy anything. I can always return a shipment and cancel at any time. Even if I never buy another book from Harlequin, the two free books and gifts are mine to keep forever.

114 HDN EEV7   314 HDN EEWK

Name	(PLEASE PRINT)	
Address		Apt.
City	State/Prov.	Zip/Postal Code

Signature (if under 18, a parent or guardian must sign)

Mail to Harlequin Reader Service®:

IN U.S.A.	**IN CANADA**
P.O. Box 1867	P.O. Box 609
Buffalo, NY	Fort Erie, Ontario
14240-1867	L2A 5X3

Not valid to current Harlequin Romance subscribers.

Want to try two free books from another line?
Call 1-800-873-8635 or visit www.morefreebooks.com.

* Terms and prices subject to change without notice. NY residents add applicable sales tax. Canadian residents will be charged applicable provincial taxes and GST. This offer is limited to one order per household. All orders subject to approval. Credit or debit balances in a customer's account(s) may be offset by any other outstanding balance owed by or to the customer. Please allow 4 to 6 weeks for delivery.

HR06

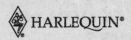
Coming Next Month

#3923 THE BRIDE OF MONTEFALCO Rebecca Winters
By Royal Appointment

Ally Parker has come to Italy with questions about her past that only Gino, duke of the aristocratic Montefalco family, can answer. Swept away to Gino's magical country estate, Ally begins to fall in love with the brooding Italian. But will the secrets and sins of the past keep Gino from making Ally the rightful bride of Montefalco...?

#3924 CRAZY ABOUT THE BOSS Teresa Southwick
The Brides of Bella Lucia

Billionaire Jack Valentine returns to London with his trusted assistant Madison Ford to make or break the Bella Lucia business. Until now, Maddy enjoyed a professional relationship with her boss. But the Jack she knew is nothing like this intoxicating man with fire in his eyes and pain in his soul. Maddy knows she could fall for him—but this Jack could easily break her heart....

#3925 CLAIMING THE CATTLEMAN'S HEART Barbara Hannay

All rugged cattle station owner Daniel Renton wants to do is build a relationship with his motherless daughter. But then newcomer Lily Halliday breezes into town like a breath of fresh air. A bond begins to form between them, but Daniel has to guard his heart and resist. Lily needs to convince Daniel to trust her—because a life with him will be worth the wait!

#3926 INHERITED: BABY Nicola Marsh

Riley Bourke is a single, successful businessman—who knows nothing about children! And Maya Edison is doing just fine on her own; she doesn't need a man to hold her hand...or a part-time father for her son. But as Riley starts to nudge his way into their hearts, Maya gives him an ultimatum: either he's *properly* part of their lives...or there's no place for him at all!